YOU GIVE ME THAT FEELING

JULIE KRISS

Copyright © 2025 by Julie Kriss

All rights reserved.

No part of this book may be reproduced in any form or by any electronic or mechanical means, including information storage and retrieval systems, without written permission from the author, except for the use of brief quotations in a book review.

ONE

Katie

THIS WAS one of the worst kisses I'd ever had, and that was saying something, because I had kissed a *lot* of men.

Charlie Mackle and I were standing in a room filled with party decorations. Streamers dangled, tinsel blinked, and a disco ball rotated where it hung from a special clamp above us. On the riser, the band had stopped playing. The other party-goers were gathered around, watching us. In a moment, they would clap.

Charlie—specifically, his character—had gone solo to his high school reunion, because the mean girl he'd dated in high school stood him up. But then I—my character—had locked eyes with him across the room. My character was the girl he'd never noticed, who had had a crush on him all these years and had tried, in several hilarious sequences, to get his attention. I got his attention in this scene by taking the stage at our high school reunion, declaring my love, and singing "Unchained

Melody." Charlie's character had then realized he was wrong all along, he'd swept me into his arms, and here we were.

He had chewed some mint gum, I'd give him that. Also, he was very good looking, with his thick, black hair swept back in a stylish cut and his expressive dark eyebrows. He wasn't a big star yet, but he was hoping for it. They all were. He might get noticed by making this Netflix romcom with me, which meant kissing me.

Wardrobe had put Charlie into a jeans-tee-and-blazer combo that was attractive and cringey at the same time. His hands on my back were icy cold. I had taken a breath mint, and right before the take, the makeup artist had sprayed setting spray directly on my mouth so my gloss wouldn't smear too much. Then it was action time, and Charlie moved in for the kill.

We'd practiced this. I angled my face just right and flung my arms around his neck. His lips were weirdly unpleasant, hard and clammy. He worked his jaw in a way I couldn't fathom, like he was chewing something. He breathed hard through his nose, and I expected a nose whistle any moment. I melted into the kiss as if I'd finally gotten the guy I'd loved for years, and he nose-breathed harder.

The tech spun the disco ball above our heads. Someone cued the extras, and they started clapping.

As rehearsed, I lifted a hand and dug it into Charlie's hair, feeling the waxy texture of layers of hair product. Once I had a grip, I kept my hand still, because it would look bad onscreen for me to muss it too much.

No one called "cut," so we had to keep going. I could hear the extras' feet shuffling on the floor.

Charlie worked his jaw some more, and then he plunged his tongue into my mouth, digging around in there like he was looking for something.

"Cut," the director said.

Charlie pulled back and grinned a wide grin. He didn't wait for director feedback. "Fantastic, babe," he said, and walked away.

I silently tamed my gag reflex as the extras stopped clapping and the set came to life around me. One of the PA's handed me a cup with a straw in it, and I grabbed it and took a gulp without caring what it might be. Diet Coke. Perfect.

The assistant director gave me a thumbs up, which meant the take was good and we didn't have to do it again. Thank God for middling streaming budgets and rapid shooting schedules that didn't allow time for a director to be fussy. You got the shot, you moved on. I swigged Diet Coke through my mouth and headed for my dressing room.

High School Reunion was my thirteenth Netflix romcom in five years, earning me the title of Romcom Queen. I had played the city girl stranded in a small town at Christmas, the American girl in England who lands a prince, and the girl who needs a date to her best friend's wedding and hires a fake boyfriend. I had been the girl who gets stuck with the cute guy at an airport in a snowstorm, and once, memorably, I had been an everyday librarian who goes back in time through a portal to the early nineteenth century, where she has to wear pretty dresses and try not to fall in love with a Regency beau. That movie was wildly popular, but the costume budget was too high, so they wouldn't let me do period pieces anymore.

I wasn't star outside of Netflix—yet—but there were Katie Armstrong fan pages and a fan site with a message board where they organized Katie Armstrong watch parties. Fans prescribed to each other which Katie Amrstrong movie to watch after a breakup or a bad day at work. They ran votes on which of my movies had the best clothes, the best hero, the best hair, the best kiss. My fans were amazing, and I didn't want to let them down, ever.

That was why *High School Reunion* worried me, and it wasn't just because of Charlie Mackle and his nose breath.

High School Reunion was about a woman in her thirties. I *was* a woman in my thirties, but still. I had three potential scripts in play as my next project, and in one of those scripts, for the first time, I would play a mom.

Certain. Death.

To be clear, I had no problems with moms. I believed fully that a woman who is a mom can also be sexy, complicated, and interesting, like a real human being. But Hollywood does *not* believe that. Mom roles were for women deemed old and sexless, given bad haircuts and high-waisted pants and absolutely no lives to live. Mom roles meant I was no longer fun romcom Katie. I was done. I needed to change direction, and fast.

In my dressing room, I grabbed my phone and sank into a chair, easing out of my high heels. No messages. I dialed my agent, Stella.

"Anything?" I asked when she answered.

"Not yet." Both of us sounded as tense as if we were counting down a NASA launch. "I've left a message, but I can't push too hard or you're out."

"Damn it."

"We can do this," Stella said. "We can. But if it doesn't happen, you'll have to choose the next project. They're waiting for your decision before anything gets greenlit."

"I can't," I said dramatically, because I could be dramatic with my agent. "The scripts are all so *bad*."

"I know, I know. But they're in talks with Jimson Greer to costar in one of them. The one where you're both teachers at the same high school and you're coaching the cheer team together."

"I can't play a cheer coach!" I protested. "I'll have to wear gym clothes and a whistle around my neck. It isn't sexy *at all.*"

None of my movies were sexy, in that they didn't have actual sex in them. Nothing ever went past a kiss. I'd never had to get naked or even show a breast. But my movies were all about chemistry and sexual tension. The kiss I'd just done with Charlie had felt weird, but it would look great onscreen. They all did, because I was a pro.

"Jimson will make it sexy," Stella said. Jimson Greer was a new up-and-coming It Boy, and by *boy* I meant he was twenty-seven. He was very pretty and very fit, but he was too young to be a cheer coach, and his name was Jimson. Could I believably make out with a guy named Jimson?

I was Katie Armstrong, so yes. Yes, I could.

"Can't Jimson do the plumber script instead?" I asked. The third script was about a rich girl (me) who inherits a house and hires a contractor to help her renovate it. The pivotal scene involved a burst sink pipe, which meant I'd get wet, and the hero would take his shirt off to fix it, and we'd almost kiss. My fans would eat it up. I could already picture how pruned and freezing I'd be on that day of shooting.

"Jimson doesn't want to do the water scene," Stella said. "He says it's exploitive. If you don't want to do the cheer coach, you might have to take the mom script. They're offering the best money for that one, and it's only five days of work."

I closed my eyes, picturing a scene in which I've cooked a huge, inexplicable breakfast (why?) and I watch in exasperation as my son rushes past it out the door to catch the school bus. "No," I groaned. "No. Call them again. He has to make a decision soon. I've auditioned three times."

I had put everyone off because I was waiting to hear about a role—*the* role. Edgar Pinsent, the Oscar-winning director, was casting for his new movie. I had flown to New York twice to audition, then to London to audition again. They made me audition in person, even though Edgar Pinsent himself wasn't there. The name of the movie was top secret, the script was under wraps, and no one auditioning was told what role they were being considered for. The whole thing was treated like a CIA black op. When you wanted a role in one of Edgar Pinsent's movies, you did what they told you and didn't ask questions.

"Katie, *no one* rushes Edgar Pinsent," Stella said. "Getting through to the assistant of his assistant is like getting through to God. I'd sell my kidney to—Oh, my God, his office is calling on the other line. I'll call you right back." She hung up.

I sat staring at the phone in my nerve-dead hand, unable to feel my face. This was it—right now. All the preparations I'd done, the auditions I'd flown to, the sleepless nights thinking about the next stage of my career, was for this. Doing this movie with Edgar Pinsent would push me to the next level—in my craft, in my level of fame, and in my finances. I would get better offers from now on if I got this. Better scripts. I would be able to spread my acting wings and do different things. I might even be able to *write* and *produce*. That thought was so heady, I couldn't even think about it too hard, like staring at the sun.

I would be able to get more money per project. I did just fine for myself, but I would be so truly rich that I could be choosy with projects instead of having to take back-to-back scripts. If this movie won Oscars—even if I didn't get one myself—it would change my life. I would never have to kiss men like Charlie Mackle ever again. I didn't even know the name of this movie, I hadn't seen the script, and I didn't know what role I might play, but I already knew that with one phone call, I would be out of the kissing game forever.

I stared at the phone as my heart pounded and my head throbbed.

There was a knock on my dressing room door. One of the assistants called, "Miss Armstrong? They need you back in makeup and on set to do pick-ups."

"Five minutes!" I called back.

I heard the assistant hesitate outside the door. He'd been given a job to do, and he was in trouble if he didn't fish me out of my dressing room. "Miss Armstrong—"

"Five minutes!" I shouted it this time, almost a bark. I was never this short with people. "Give me five freaking minutes! I have diarrhea!"

That shut him up. I heard his footsteps moving away.

I got up and paced. If I got this role, I promised the universe, I would be a good person. I was already a good person, but I would be even better. I would do even more free appearances to promote animal rescue charities. I already did a few a year, but I would do more, and I would promote other things, too. Cancer charities. The Red Cross. Did they need me to fly somewhere and look pensive while wearing well-tailored fatigues? I could do that. I could—

My phone buzzed, and I almost dropped it. I juggled it and punched the answer button. "Stella!" I shouted into the phone.

"Okay, honey, calm down," Stella said. She was only five years older than me, but when she used her motherly energy, it was unmatched. "Everything is under control."

"What's going on?" I shouted into the piece of plastic in my hand. Why were phones so small and insignificant? Big moments called for old-fashioned phones with big handsets. It was hard to be dramatic with this thing.

"He's still undecided," Stella said. "You aren't out of the running yet. But, Katie, I'll be honest. Edgar Pinsent told his assistant—who told *his* assistant, who told me—that he has doubts."

I froze in my pacing, trying to process this. "What kind of doubts? I'll do coaching sessions. Does he need an accent? I'll master it, even Australian. I'll lose weight. Or gain weight. I'll dye my hair. I'll shave it. Stella, I can *do* this."

"I know you can, honey," Stella said, and for the first time I heard her hesitate. "Edgar says he isn't sure because you're too sweet."

We were both silent for a breath.

"This is fixable," Stella said into the silence. She sounded confident. "He's looking at your reel, and all he sees are romcoms. Your auditions are great, but he doesn't know you like I do. He sees what the public sees, and you're gorgeous and wonderful, but he's looking for dark and edgy. You know?"

"I'm too sweet," I said slowly.

"Yes. But we can *fix* it. You can pick up some indie roles. We'll get you booked to some late-night talk shows, and we'll write raunchy stories to tell to show your other side. I'll call a stylist to change up your look."

I shook my head. "A new look? Stella, I'm not Sandy in *Grease*. A perm and some fake leather pants won't get me a role with Edgar Pinsent. And taking indie roles will take time. We don't have time."

"Yes, we do," she said. "The funding for the movie is being renegotiated, so the project is on hold for three months. Edgar is going to take a retreat in Romania to revise the script. The casting is on hold. I'm telling you, Katie, you aren't out of this. Not yet. What did Winston Churchill say?"

I knew the answer, because this was one of Stella's rallying cries, even though Winston Churchill was talking about a world war, not getting roles in Hollywood. "'Never, ever, ever give up,'" I quoted.

"That's right. We have three months to prove to Edgar Pinsent that you're more than just the pretty girl next door. I've been thinking about this, anyway—you've needed to change your image for a while. I've come up with several possible strategies."

"Wait a minute. You agree with Edgar Pinsent? You think I'm too sweet?"

"Katie," Stella said in her version of a kind, gentle voice, "the word *edgy* isn't one that anyone associates with you. I love you, but you know that."

I stood straighter. "I'm edgy," I argued. "I wore a miniskirt in *Party of Two*. And I showed my bra."

"It was a bra strap," Stella corrected me. "You showed a bra strap. Middle school kids have seen more than that. You've never even worn a bathing suit onscreen."

It was true, I hadn't. I had never seen the need, and my fans weren't asking for it. But whatever I was doing wasn't working anymore. Maybe I should start thinking outside of my routine. "Okay, I'm listening. What are your ideas?"

"I could get you an erotic script," Stella said. "Which would mean nudity."

My hand flew to my lower belly and instinctively felt the shape of it. I kept fit, but there was a difference between *fit* and *nude scene fit*. "I'm not in training," I hedged. "I'd need two months to be ready for a nude scene, and Edgar Pinsent won't see the movie in time."

"A fair point," she said grudgingly. "You'd have to tone up and drop twenty pounds."

My face went hot. "Jeez, Stella. Not twenty. Ten."

"Fifteen," she shot back, because negotiating was in her blood. "Still, the timeline won't work. No problem. If you can't show some tits and ass to look edgy, then I have another idea.

One that doesn't need you to diet, and we can put it in place right away."

"What is it?" I tried not to sound too eager to do whatever it took to keep my clothes on.

I could hear Stella's triumphant smile through the phone. "If they want your wild side, we're going to bring some wild into your life. We're getting you a boyfriend."

TWO

Travis

SOMEONE WAS CALLING ME.

I stared at the water, transfixed. Clear pool water, crisp and clean. It looked blue because the inside of the pool was blue. It looked serene and peaceful. The sun caught the surface, sending up sparks of light. I stared.

"Travis," someone said.

The air brushed my skin, a warm California breeze. The water would be cool, though. I could just lean further, then further still, and then I would be falling. Straight down. Maybe I could keep my eyes open as I fell.

"Travis."

Would I feel better under the water, in the cool silence? Or would I just drown?

The voice got closer and sharper. "Hey, kid. You're naked."

I blinked, focusing my eyes. I knew I was naked. My feet

were bare where I stood at the edge of this diving board, my legs too. The warm breeze touched all of my skin, everywhere.

If I tilted face-first into the pool, I'd feel the water all over. It was my favorite way to swim.

"Travis." It was Andy's voice, moving from concerned to annoyed. I heard him snap his fingers. "Are you there? Put your junk away, kid. There's someone here to see you."

I blinked again. My eyes were dry. I wasn't a kid. I was a man, I was standing naked on a diving board over a pool, and someone was here to see me?

"I'm not expecting anyone," I said, still staring at my bare feet. They were nice feet, actually. Well shaped. They were evenly tanned, too, like the rest of me. I spent a lot of time out by this pool.

"You are expecting someone," Andy argued. "I told you about it before. They're in the house waiting for you right now. These women don't want to see your dong, kid, and neither do I. So put it away. It's gonna get sunburned, just waving around like that."

I finally raised my head and looked at Andy. He was standing at the edge of the pool. Andy was sixty-five, and this was his L.A. mansion, where I'd been staying for six months, because I had nowhere else to go.

Ever since my world-famous band had broken up, my career had crashed, and lawsuits had drained me of most of my money, I had been homeless. The Malibu house I'd owned was the first thing to go, with all of the money going to debts and lawyer bills. Then the New York apartment was sold. I suddenly had no fixed address.

At thirty-two, after touring the world for ten years, I was living on an allowance allotted by my lawyer that could barely cover rent in L.A. I was lucky to afford the rented storage unit that contained most of my belongings. My assistants and hangers-on had vanished. My former bandmates hated me. As I fell from the top all the way down to the bottom, my so-called friends and many acquaintances had been conspicuously silent.

I had been looking for an apartment, quietly spiraling, wondering if I could sleep in the storage unit without getting caught, when Andy Rockweller called me.

Andy had been the lead singer of a huge hit band in the eighties. Back then, he'd dyed his hair bright purple and worn it in gelled spikes, and he'd always performed in an all-leather outfit, including a leather shirt with a leather vest over it. It was a lot of leather, but Andy Rockweller had pulled it off. I had met him a few times at parties over the years—parties at which he was sober and I was various levels of wasted. Still, we'd hit it off, and at some point I'd given him my number. When he heard how badly off I was, he'd called and offered me a place to stay.

Today, he wore chino pants, a short-sleeved button-down shirt, and Birkenstocks, and his long gray hair was woven in a neat braid down his back. He might not wear all that leather anymore, but even with crinkles at the corners of his eyes and a graying beard, he gave off rock star energy. He was just that guy.

I wasn't sure why he had taken me in. We weren't related. He didn't need my money. We had been barely acquainted when he invited me. He'd said that since his last divorce, his mansion was too big for one person, and he wouldn't mind a roommate, as long as I didn't mess the place up. I'd wondered at the time if he wanted sex, but six months in, I knew that wasn't the case, either. Andy Rockweller was firmly straight, and even at his age, he could—and did—get laid whenever he wanted. He didn't need me for that.

I frowned at him, trying to remember when he'd told me someone was coming over. A woman. More than one woman?

He sighed. I wasn't high or hungover, and he knew it. I was just... absent. I was like that a lot over the past year. Days could go by while I stared at the pool. Being absent was quiet. It was peaceful. It was my preferred state of mind. It was—

"Put. Your. Pecker. Away," Andy said slower, as if English was my second language.

My gaze moved behind his shoulder to the house. The floor-to-ceiling windows that looked out to the pool had no blinds on them. I was probably fully visible to whoever was in there. I sighed and walked reluctantly off the diving board, heading for the beach towel I'd dropped over a chair.

"Towel's not good enough," Andy interrupted me. "Put on clothes."

He unfolded the cloth I hadn't noticed tucked under his arm. He held out a pair of shorts and a T-shirt, which he must have taken from my room.

I grabbed the shorts. I was starting to be present again, and I didn't like it. "This better be good," I said as I stepped into them, commando. When I pulled them up, Andy gave me a look that said, *Finally*.

"It's good," he said. He waved the shirt at me, but I ignored it. I slid my feet into the flip-flops I'd left on the pool deck. "You agreed to it."

"Is it a lawyer?" I asked. I'd had dozens of lawyer appointments. I had no desire to look any kind of respectable for a lawyer, even a female one. She could look at my tats just like everyone else.

"Not a lawyer." Andy was firm. He stepped in front of me and pushed the shirt at my chest, wedging it there. His expression said that I wasn't getting past him. "Kid, put this on. And behave."

"What for?" I asked, taking the shirt from him and pulling it over my head.

"Your big chance."

I laughed out loud at that. "I've heard that before. I remember one guy promising me *my big chance* when I was twenty. He tried to fuck me twenty minutes later."

"No one is fucking you except for yourself," Andy said. "Now go be nice, and pay attention, because this is good. Have I ever led you wrong?"

I ran my hands through my hair, trying to neaten it a little, because yeah, I had to admit, he had never led me wrong. If Andy wanted me to do this, whatever it was, then I'd try it. For a few minutes, at least.

I just wished I could remember what he'd told me about it, because I had no idea what this was.

He slid open the glass door, and when my eyes adjusted, I saw there was no one in the sitting room. Whoever was here hadn't seen me naked, at least. Andy led me down the hall to the huge kitchen, which contained a dining table that could easily seat six people and didn't have a view to the pool.

I blinked at the people sitting at the table. A red-haired woman wearing tortoiseshell glasses and typing intensely on her phone. A Korean guy in an open-throat dress shirt who looked like he could be a model. And a second woman, who was wearing large sunglasses and a blue scarf over her head, tied under her chin. Indoors. I saw a glimpse of dark hair and her naturally red lips, and that was all.

I couldn't figure out the disguised lady, so I turned to the Korean guy, who was the only person I recognized. "Jon?" I said.

Jonathan Kim, my new agent, gave me a brief, sharp nod. "Hi, Travis. Glad you could make it."

It was a dig, even though he said it politely. Since my old agent had screwed me over so badly I was homeless, Andy had introduced me to Jon. Andy knew everyone in the music business, and he vouched for Jon, so I had agreed to meet him. We'd talked for ten minutes, after which we shook hands, and apparently, I had a new agent. I didn't bother to feel bad that there was no work for him to agent for me. Anyone taking me on in the middle of my current, well-publicized nosedive probably knew he wasn't going to make any money.

Since that ten-minute conversation, I hadn't spoken to Jon again. I scratched the back of my neck, once again wishing I'd paid attention whenever Andy had told me what this meeting was. "What's going on?" I asked.

"Take a seat," Jon said, reaching out the toe of one impeccable dress shoe and pushing an empty chair toward me.

I reluctantly sat. I looked at the scarf-and-sunglasses woman again. She seemed to be looking at me, but it was impossible to tell. I could only see my own reflection in the lenses of her glasses.

"Anyone want a lemonade?" Andy asked, walking toward the fridge.

No one else answered, but I was thirsty. "I do," I said.

There was another second of silence as Andy opened the fridge. Was the air conditioning always this cold? I rubbed my arms, missing the burning heat outside. The scarf-and-sunglasses woman seemed to watch me.

Finally, the redhead finished typing and put her phone down on the table with a smack. "Nice job introducing us," she snapped at Jon, and then she turned to me. "Travis. Hi. I'm Stella Green." She held out a hand.

I shook it. It was cold, and suddenly I was all the way back into my head, back into my life. I didn't remember what this meeting was, but it didn't matter. The fact that these people were here could only mean they wanted something from me. Otherwise, why had they set up a meeting and come all the way to Andy's house? People didn't do that when they wanted to give you something. They did that when they wanted to take.

I ran through the usual suspects of things people had wanted from me over my years in the music business. Money? I didn't have much left. Sex? My agent wouldn't be here for that. Music? My band was finished, and no one gave a shit about me without them.

"My client and I appreciate your time," Stella Green said. I leaned back in my chair, crossing my arms and looking at the scarf-and-sunglasses woman again. She must be famous. That had to be it. I turned back to Stella.

"No problem," I said.

Andy put my lemonade in front of me, and I picked it up and sipped it. It was icy and delicious. Stella turned to Jon again. "How much have you told him?" she asked.

"Nothing," Jon replied.

"Seriously? You couldn't have given him the basics?"

"I wanted to hear you pitch it."

"Of course you did." Her tone was scathing. She turned back to me. "Sorry about this, Travis. Your agent was supposed to prep you."

"I'm the reason you have this meeting at all," Jon shot back.

"Then if you aren't going to help, be quiet and let me talk."

"Please," Jon said to her. "Go ahead. We're both listening."

Stella sighed. "Katie has an unusual situation. I'm a big fan of Seven Dog Down, so when I thought of solutions to her problem, your name came into my head. I think that the two of you could help each other out." She glanced at the scarf woman, who I assumed must be Katie. I didn't know of anyone famous named Katie. Stella continued on. "We came here today on the understanding that everyone here agrees to be discreet. Nothing we discuss today leaves this room, even if we can't make a deal, and—"

"Stella, enough." The scarf-and-sunglasses woman spoke for the first time. Her voice was tense. She turned to me. "Mr. White, I'm sorry for how weird this is."

While I tried to process being called *Mr. White*, she took off the sunglasses and tugged off the scarf, revealing gray eyes, dark brown hair in soft waves, and a heart-shaped face with a perfect chin. She was gorgeous. I had never seen her before in my life.

"I had to wear this," she said, gesturing to the scarf, "just in case anyone spotted me coming here today. I didn't want to be recognized. My name is Katie Armstrong. Do you ever watch Netflix?"

"Not really," I said.

Katie nodded, and her cheeks turned pink. "Okay, um. I'm an actress, and I'm on there a lot. I'm really, *really* sorry to bother you with this." She pinched the bridge of her nose in embarrassment. "Stella, this is *totally* out of line."

"It isn't," Stella reassured her. "Go ahead."

Katie sighed and dropped her hand. "I need a boyfriend," she blurted.

I felt my eyebrows go up. I should probably feel surprise at some point in the rest of my life, but today was not that day. "Yeah?" I asked.

"I know you're busy," Katie plowed on, ignoring the fact that I very obviously wasn't busy. "And I know that this is going to seem strange, but there are reasons, and we discussed it, and —this all sounded so reasonable in my head an hour ago."

I looked at the faces around the table, taking this in. Andy was in the kitchen somewhere behind me, lounging against the counter and probably being wildly entertained. I scratched my chin.

"Anyone want to elaborate?" I asked the room.

Stella leaned forward. "We propose that the two of you have a relationship—a fake one, of course. We'll set up photo ops for the two of you to be seen together. Katie and I have a script."

"A script?" I looked at Jon. He shrugged.

"I've read it," he said. "It looked good to me."

I narrowed my gaze on him. I knew about fake relationships—everyone in Hollywood did. Getting photographed with another famous person as if the two of you were dating was a great way to get free exposure and publicity for both of you. I had never done the fake thing myself, but the idea didn't shock me.

What surprised me was that everyone in this room thought that this was a good idea for me. That this woman—Katie Armstrong—was a good idea for me.

"Jon," I said.

Jon held up his hands. "Hear us out. Katie is an excellent actress with a great reputation. She could redeem you in the eyes of the public. Get your career going again."

Redeem. Right. I hadn't exactly had a great year. Or a great eighteen months, if you wanted to split hairs. When Seven Dog Down ended and my life crashed, well...mistakes were made. By me. In public.

Still, redemption hadn't crossed my mind. That I needed it. That it was even possible if I did. That I would care enough to try. Reviving my career hadn't crossed my mind, either. All I'd wanted for a while now was to sit by Andy's pool and stare at the water, thinking about the color blue.

I realized the table was silent because they were waiting for a reaction from me. They thought I might take offense to the idea that I needed redeeming. No one at this table was sure of exactly what I would do—rage? Laugh? Weep? Walk away? None of them knew me, except Andy a little bit. I didn't even know myself anymore.

If I were smart, I would ask questions. There were a lot of

them. Why had they come to me with this? Why did this Katie woman need a boyfriend? Why couldn't she get one for herself? Why did she need a team of professionals, and why had they all picked me? Why would I bother redeeming myself to anyone? What was in it for her? What was in it for me? Was there money in this deal? If so, who was paying, her or me?

Could I fake date a woman? This woman? Could I do it convincingly?

I took another look at Katie. Her ribcage wasn't moving—she was literally holding her breath. She looked terrified, but she was also gorgeous, because of course she was. She was an actress.

Date a hot woman and make it look real? Who did they think they were talking to? I'd do it for free, just because it would fuck with people. It turned out I had no questions at all.

I smiled at Katie, and when I spoke, it was directly to her. "All right," I said. "When do we start?"

THREE

Katie

I WAS FROZEN in my chair in this very nice kitchen. I was a professional actress. I had started in theater and improv. It had been years since I had missed a cue or forgotten a line. And right now, the entire script had left my head, possibly forever.

Travis White—world famous rock star, sex god, lead singer of Seven Dog Down, a man whose music I had listened to and who I had drooled over in countless TikToks, because of course I had a top secret TikTok account—was smiling *right at me*. And he was...agreeing?

He was even better looking in person. I hadn't thought that was possible, but here we were. His dark blond hair was bed-tousled, from an actual bed and not from a stylist. His eyes weren't just blue, they were cerulean, or turquoise, or something else wildly poetic. His face was perfectly shaped, with high cheekbones and a flawless jaw, but the appeal of Travis

White had never been that he was something as simple as handsome. His appeal was in the wild air about him, the sexy and knowing look in his eyes, the slashes of his brows.

Travis White wasn't the nice guy who would take you on a date to Olive Garden. He wasn't the guy who ran the Christmas tree farm or the royal prince who marries an everyday girl or the guy you kissed at your high school reunion.

No, he looked exactly like a guy who would throw you on the back of his bike, drive you for hours, then set up camp at sundown and screw you in a sleeping bag, and you'd love every dirty, windblown minute of it. You'd be on your deathbed sixty years later, surrounded by your loving husband and your precious grandchildren, remembering that guy who'd fucked you silly in a sleeping bag and thinking, *Damn, I had a good life.*

I had been speechless even before he entered the room, because as we were sitting down, Andy Rockweller had gone out back to retrieve Travis, and we had all heard him say, *Hey, kid. You're naked.*

I had made a small sound in my throat, and my knees had given out as I sank into a chair. I was still wearing the scarf and sunglasses I'd put on to be incognito, and I hadn't been able to lift my hands to remove them. It was like I'd been hit over the head in an old cartoon. Stella had been too busy texting to pay attention, and Jonathan Kim had only rolled his eyes in annoyance.

Then Travis White had walked into the kitchen, no longer naked, wearing low-hanging shorts and a worn T-shirt. He had dressed so quickly that I was suddenly sure he hadn't put any underwear on under those shorts. He had been naked a minute ago, twenty feet away. Honestly, I was nothing more than a straight woman on planet Earth, so I'd had to take a few minutes to recover from that fact while I hid behind my sunglasses.

While Stella and Jonathan had sniped at each other, Travis had rubbed his arms, and my gaze followed his hands, hypnotized. A tattoo of a snake wound over his left forearm. The snake's head was placed on Travis's wrist, its eye dark and gleaming against Travis's golden tan. Travis's hands were capable musician's hands, and I heard the soft rasp of his palms rubbing his own skin. I thought I might be pregnant.

This meeting was going all wrong, though. I'd thought the idea was crazy when Stella first mentioned it, but Stella was a great agent because she was an incredible saleswoman. She'd convinced me that not only was this idea good, it was *essential*. The only way to get the role in Edgar Pinsent's next movie was to have a fake, wild fling with Travis White, and Stella had connections to get a meeting with him. She said that if we could get him to agree, it would be easy from there. We even came up with a script.

When I came to my senses in the middle of this meeting—when the words *I need a boyfriend* had unbelievably come out of my mouth—I had wanted nothing more than to slide under this table and pretend I no longer existed. The embarrassment was immense. I had begun to wonder where the farthest point on earth was from this very spot, and how quickly I could go there. Did they take just anyone at research bases in Antarctica? Where could I buy a coat? How soon could I get a flight?

Then Travis had smiled at me and said he would do it.

Why? I wondered past the screeching in my head. He hadn't asked any questions. He didn't even know who I *was*. I should probably be offended by that, but in the moment, I was only grateful. If Travis White forgot my name five minutes after this disaster of a meeting was over, it would be merciful for all of us.

His blue—cerulean! azure!—eyes were mesmerizing as they fixed on me, and his smile was so effortlessly cocky that it should have been fake but it wasn't. His posture was relaxed in his chair, his hand curled on the table. He wasn't tense or forced into this. He wasn't shocked. He wasn't drunk or high. He was just...agreeing, and I didn't know why, and suddenly I couldn't let him do it.

"Don't," I said, surprising all of us. Jonathan's eyebrows went up. Beside me, Stella went so tense I practically felt vibrations through the floor. Behind Travis, Andy Rockweller watched the scene and sipped his lemonade, the corners of his eyes crinkling.

This felt good, felt right for the first time in this meeting, so I said it again. "Travis, don't do it. Don't say yes."

Travis's smile had faded and he cocked his head, ignoring everyone but me. "You think so? Why?"

"Because it's a bad idea."

"I like bad ideas," Travis shot back. "They're my favorite kind."

Beside me, I heard Stella whisper under her breath, "My god, he's perfect."

"This one's really bad," I persisted. "We can't pull it off."

His voice dropped just low enough to vibrate. "Oh, I can pull it off."

My breath choked in my throat.

"I'm a fucking genius," Stella whispered to herself.

Travis's gaze still hadn't left my face. "Can't you do it?" he asked me. "I thought you were an actress."

"I am. But doesn't this seem crazy to you?" I gestured around me, to the others in the room. "Stella and I drank wine the other night and wrote a script." I pulled a wad of folded-up pages from my handbag and smoothed them out. "It has three acts. The first meeting and the first dates, the middle part of the relationship, and then the breakup." I waved the pages at him, trying to emphasize my point.

"There are lines, settings, and stage directions. A complete fantasy relationship between you and me. Doesn't that seem *nuts* to you? You should be calling the police, not talking to us."

Travis held out his hand. "Let me see." When I hesitated, his brows lowered. "Everyone in this room has read this script except for me. Even Andy. Right, Andy?"

"I read it," Andy replied from his spot leaning against the kitchen counter. "It's a humdinger."

"It seems I'm the last one left in the dark," Travis said without glancing at Andy. He still held out his hand. "I might be somewhat deserving of being treated like a child, I admit, but it ends now. I'd like to see the script."

He talked like this sometimes, I knew. He was capable of elaborate sentences that he'd sprinkle into conversation, because yes, I had watched interviews with Travis White.

I handed over the pages, and he took them, shuffling them together. He started at page one and leafed through. The silence was heavy in the room.

"We meet at a Lakers game," he commented without looking up.

"Courtside seats," I croaked. "We're randomly placed next to each other when someone swaps their tickets with us."

"So we're on camera when we meet, and everyone sees us. That's pretty good."

I pushed down the glow I felt at his approval. The Lakers game was my idea, partly lifted from a romcom I'd done in which the hero had proposed on the jumbo screen at a sports event in the climactic moment.

Travis turned a page. Even scruffy and unkempt, there was no other word for Travis—he was golden. His skin had a radiant glow, his hair a sun-kissed shine. He was clean shaven, and he wore no jewelry, not even rock star rings. He'd truly been naked when we arrived—so naked that he had tanned evenly all over. I felt my cheeks flushing hot.

"A restaurant date," Travis commented, flipping another page. "Then a breakfast date. Cheeky."

"The implications, you know," I said weakly. The idea was that Good Girl Katie had done the unthinkable and hooked up with a hot rock star.

"I get it," he said, flipping the page casually, as if he read scripts of fake sex hookups with strangers every day. "Shopping trips. A weekend in Cabo."

"We don't have to do that one if you don't want," I said hurriedly. Stella kicked me under the table. The Cabo trip was her idea, and we had hotly debated it. Stella insisted that pictures of me and Travis frolicking on the beach would be irresistible. *Everyone does it! It's sexy!* That was her argument.

My argument was that I'd have to wear a bathing suit for that, and we were doing this to avoid me needing to get naked in public. Even though I had never looked closely at my own butt, I knew there was jiggle in it.

Travis shrugged and said, "I don't mind," because he was not only perfect, he was a man, and butt jiggles had never occurred to him. Life was unfair.

He flipped another page. "Premiere or awards show optional," he read.

"It depends how it's going," I explained. "People might like to see us dressed up."

He frowned for the first time, as if this concerned him. "I'm not invited to any awards shows right now. And I'm definitely not nominated."

I laughed. "I'm never nominated. I make romcoms. According to awards shows, my genre doesn't exist, and even if it does, it requires no acting talent."

"Awards are overrated," Travis said with a shrug. "We got a Grammy once."

"For *The Serpent* soundtrack," I said.

He raised his gaze from the script, and we locked eyes. He was surprised that I knew that.

"I saw the movie," I said lamely. "It was a great soundtrack."

Travis frowned slowly, as if I had said something in another language. He didn't even thank me for the compliment. "We can do an awards show if you want. Or a premiere." His tone was reluctant.

"Like I say, we'll see how it's going," I told him. "Assuming we actually do this, of course."

"We're doing it," Travis said. Behind him, Andy grinned like this was making his day.

When Travis flipped the script closed and dropped it on the table, I protested. "You haven't read the last part. The part about our breakup."

"Is it bad?" he asked. "Am I a dick in the breakup?"

"Of course not. We get seen separately a few times, and then we split amicably and give statements that we grew apart and we'll always be friends. Why would I make you a dick in the breakup?"

"To make yourself look good. Making me look like a dick is easy."

I had seen the headlines about his bad behavior lately—fistfights and a wrecked hotel room. "This is supposed to benefit you," I said, pointing at the script, "just as much as it benefits me."

He cocked his head. "And how, exactly, does all of this benefit you, Katie? What do you get out of breakfast dates and fake hookups with me?"

I had honestly forgotten the other people in the room. They

were figments of imagination. There was only Travis, with his wild attractiveness and his magnetism and his *everything*. My embarrassment burned away when I realized truly, deep down, that he was right for this. This whole crazy idea was somehow right.

"I get a ticket out of romcom land," I told him, leaning forward. "I get to be seen as a three-dimensional woman instead of a goody-two-shoes cartoon. I'm tired of playing the girl who only wants the shirtless contractor to notice her or the cute lumberjack to kiss her. I want to do something out of character. I want to be sexy and unpredictable and hot. And if you help me be those things—even if it's fake—I just *might* get taken seriously in this business."

The blue of his eyes blazed right into me, straight through me as I said this speech. I didn't want to sink under the table anymore. I locked eyes with him and stared back.

When he spoke, his voice was low, like he was speaking only to me, even though the others in the room could hear. "So you want to be bad," he said.

"Yes," I shot back.

"You're on."

Next to me, Stella smacked her palm lightly on the table. "Thank God," she said. "We have a deal."

FOUR

Travis

AS PART of his conditions of my staying with him, Andy forbade me from smoking, so I had the Ferris wheel of nicotine withdrawal to dominate the amusement park of my ruined life. Andy was also sober after partying hard through the early nineties, and though his rules about that weren't as strict, I abstained out of respect. It helped to have a clear head to navigate the shitshow.

But I couldn't completely raw dog life at the moment, so the day after the meeting with Katie Armstrong, I popped a weed gummy in Andy's basement TV room and turned on Netflix.

Andy found me four hours later, wrapped in a blanket next to an empty bowl of popcorn, watching my third Katie Armstrong movie in a row. I barely acknowledged him when he came in. In this movie, Katie was a small-town bakery owner, and a country music star had come to town to shoot a music video. The scene onscreen featured a flour accident in Katie's bakery, and the country music star—who had carefully curated scruff, highlighted hair, and veneers you could see from space—was wiping flour from the tip of her nose.

"I couldn't find you when you weren't by the pool," Andy said, dropping into one of the room's plush chairs. This basement was nicer than any of my apartments growing up, with a huge screen and multiple seats that were deliriously comfortable. My second gummy kicked in, and my body made a bid to become one with the sofa as my mind processed the movie.

"I'm working," I said.

Andy let those words float for a minute, since it was obvious to both of us that I was watching Netflix stoned. "Right. So what's the verdict?"

I pointed at Katie onscreen. "She's good. Really good." I moved my pointer finger to indicate the hero. "He's supposed to be a musician, but when they showed him playing guitar, he was holding the fretboard with all his fingers, like a fist."

"The hell you say." Andy put his feet up, and the scene shifted to Katie's apartment, where she was cleaning herself up after the flour incident. She changed out of her baker's whites into a pretty dress, then looked at herself in the bathroom mirror and shook her head. "What am I thinking? He'd never notice a girl like me," she said to herself onscreen.

"She's pretty," Andy commented.

"She's beautiful," I replied. "She's funny. She has flawless comic timing. She can act. She can sing and dance. She looks good in everything."

"So you like her," Andy said.

"What's not to like?" Katie was sexy, too, though I didn't say that aloud. It was in the tilt of her chin, her thick lashes, the way she could cock her hip when she wasn't pretending to be clumsy. She had a body that wouldn't quit. "She's literally perfect," I said. "I've never seen a more perfect woman. But she's right. She's *too* perfect, and these movies are okay, but she could do better."

"And yet, you're still watching," Andy observed.

Onscreen, the cowboy kissed Katie. I couldn't help the disgusted sound I made. "He's supposed to be a musician?" I heckled the TV. "We kiss *way* better than that."

Andy said something else, but I wasn't listening. I was watching the kiss. I didn't like it. This was the third guy I'd seen her kiss today, and even though I didn't know Katie, I was becoming an expert at how she kissed men.

She was good at it. Professional. She knew how to angle her head, where to place her hands. The sides of the guy's neck, or in his hair, or on his shoulders with her fingers digging in. She knew how to look lost in the moment, like this guy's presence was carrying her away. She knew how to press against him just enough to be suggestive without being dirty. When Katie Armstrong kissed a man, she knew exactly what she was doing.

It was the men who were the problem. One guy had been so Botoxed it must have felt like kissing wax. The men put their hands on her waist or placed them weirdly on her jaw. This cowboy had his lips pinched closed and was letting Katie do all the work. Katie was a good kisser, and she was wasted on every single one of these deadbeats. Had she ever been kissed properly, even once?

Something switched on in my brain. I felt the pop of disused electrical wires firing up.

I could kiss her better than those guys had. I could kiss her better than all of them.

"Travis." Andy's voice was harsh, as if he'd said my name more than once. I glanced over at him.

"What?" I asked.

"Don't fuck this up. Bad ideas, remember?" he said. "You've been having a lot of them."

I scoffed and looked back at the screen. I had punched my former agent—who had been robbing me for years—and gotten an assault charge. Then I had skipped a court appearance to go to New Orleans, and...Okay, I was impulsive, and all of that was a bad idea. But like I'd told Katie, bad ideas were my favorite kind.

I watched Katie as the cowboy's ex-girlfriend—who was skinny and evil, of course—came into the bakery, unaware that the sweet, small-town baker had kissed her ex. The evil ex-girlfriend was talking loudly about getting her boyfriend back. Katie looked down, quietly crushed.

I wouldn't sleep with her. That wasn't in the deal, and besides, my dick had been in cold storage for months. I couldn't remember the last time I'd felt genuinely aroused by anything—not porn, not real-life women, not even my own hand. My body was taking a perma-nap from the waist down. Depression? Anxiety? Stress? Crushing self-doubt? Apocalyptic lack of belief in a future that contained any form of happiness or fulfillment? Take your pick from the buffet, or have a little bit of everything.

I wasn't going to see her naked, and that was fine. But I *could* mess her up a little. Like she'd asked me to.

"I liked her," Andy said. "She's a nice girl. I don't want to see her hurt." We were quiet as in the movie, the cowboy had dinner with his ex-girlfriend, supposedly to talk things out. It was inevitable that Katie would see them in the restaurant and get the wrong idea.

"Let them get back together," I heckled the TV. "They deserve each other."

"Both of the agents asked me if you've been using," Andy said.

I frowned. The question was more annoying than offensive. "I'm not. I quit two years ago."

Even if I felt like lying to Andy—which I didn't—there was no point. No one knew more about drug use than Andy Rockweller. If I had scored, if I had done anything stronger than these weed gummies in the six months I'd lived here, he would know.

Personally, I had been more of a recreational user. I tried whatever came my way—and in the music business, quite a bit came your way. Drugs were fun, but they never scratched my particular itch, and eventually I gave up out of boredom. It was a hobby that cost a lot of money, so you had to be all in.

"They were just doing their due diligence," Andy said. "I told them that you're not using. I would know if you were. I told them you're basically a good kid who's had some bad breaks lately, and you haven't handled it well. I told them that being around a nice girl would do you good. And reviving your career wouldn't be the worst thing, either."

I squinted at him. Andy was hard to read, and it was especially hard with my IQ lowered.

"Wait a second," I said, slow on the uptake. "You *didn't* tell me about the meeting beforehand. That's why I didn't remember it was happening."

Andy's gaze moved innocently away. "I might have said something."

"No, you didn't. You sprung that meeting on me. I never agreed to it." I sat up—a few inches up, anyway. "Tell me the truth. Did you set it up because you want me out of your house? You should have said something if you do."

"I like having you here," Andy protested. "You're low maintenance. It's like having an animated houseplant."

That really should have offended me, but—fuck. I *was* an animated houseplant these days. I used to go onstage and rip up tens of thousands of fans as an average day. I traveled the world and dated beautiful women. Sure, I hated my band, the music sucked, and a lot of the time I'd been miserable and/or loaded, but at least I'd done something with my life.

I glanced back at the movie. Katie had indeed seen the veneer guy with his ex, and she had closed her bakery and was about to drive out of town. What woman would close down her whole business over a dude? It made no sense. I didn't have to watch the rest, because I already knew the ending, and suddenly, that didn't cut it.

"This story is too predictable," I said.

"It's just a movie," Andy said.

"Not the movie. Well, yes—the movie. But I meant the script Katie wrote. It wasn't exciting enough. It was tame. I already knew the ending."

"I don't like the sound of that," Andy said.

"Too late. You got me into this." I smiled at him. "This script is going to have a plot twist. And I've decided I'm going to write it."

FIVE

Katie

I HAD LISTENED to Seven Dog Down over the years. Everyone had, because they were hard to escape. Their music was on commercials and movie soundtracks. The five members of Seven Dog Down were celebrities and sex symbols. Their tours were sold out. Then, two years ago, the band broke up.

The stories that came out after that got weirder and darker. The band had sued their management and their record company for screwing them over, which led to countersuits. The band members had nothing good to say about each other in interviews. Seven Dog Down's guitarist had referred to Travis White as "fucking deranged," and Travis had responded in his own interview by saying, "If you'd had to spend ten years trapped with those guys, you'd be fucking deranged, too."

It was nasty. And then Travis had made it worse.

His pop-star girlfriend, Sabrina Lowe, had broken up with him, saying she "wished him well," which is PR codespeak for

He's an asshole. Travis hadn't badmouthed Sabrina—thank God—but he *had* punched his former agent in a fistfight in his front yard in Malibu, which had gotten him an assault charge. Then he'd skipped his court appearance for the assault and had turned up in New Orleans to drunkenly trash his hotel room and rack up a second charge for disorderly conduct.

He hadn't denied any of it or tried to cover it up. He hadn't blamed anyone else. He'd made all of his mistakes in public, where anyone could see them. I didn't know whether this made him honest or not very smart. It didn't matter, because he was perfect.

I wasn't a sports girl, and this was my first Lakers game, but that was part of the story. Stella and Jonathan had organized the tickets, and all I knew was that I'd taken a friend's ticket last minute when they couldn't make the game. It was out of character for me, a moment when I impulsively tried something new. When Travis and I would later tell the story of our meet cute, we wouldn't have to stray far from the truth.

I had dressed carefully in jeans and a casual tee, my hair in a ponytail. I wore sneakers and my everyday makeup, because I was just a single girl having a night out, unaware she was about to meet the man who would sweep her away. I took a selfie and posted it to Instagram—*Off to my first ever basketball game! Go Lakers!*—and it got over a thousand likes in the first five minutes. I was *ready.*

Travis was late.

As the first period played out in front of me, I kept my eyes on the game. I clapped and cheered, but inside I started to boil. Where was he? Stella told me he'd been given all the details— we'd used intermediaries because when we exchanged numbers tonight, I wanted it to look real. It wouldn't be real if I already had Travis's number and was texting him before he even arrived.

There were always celebrities at a Lakers game, which meant there were always press and people celebrity-watching at a Lakers game. I wasn't treated like a big deal, but I could tell in the air around me that some people knew me. The reality of being a celebrity in the age of cell phones and social media is that when you're in public you always have to assume that someone, somewhere is taking a picture or a video of you. It isn't the old days of paparazzi chasing you down. Instead, every person you see when you step out the door is paparazzi. All the time.

So I didn't want to restlessly check my phone for messages from Stella. I wanted to stay in character. But the later it got, the more I fumed. I was going to give in and pull out my phone when I heard a murmur in the crowd around me.

It was like an ocean wave rolling through everyone—people shifting in their seats, turning, their attention moving. This was an L.A. crowd impossible to impress, and yet people were craning their necks, because Travis White was making an entrance.

An usher directed him down the row of seats, but instead of being annoyed, everyone he stepped over seemed delighted. People grinned up at him as they moved their knees. They fist-bumped him and said hi. And I watched in awe as Travis White, the rock star, dazzled them without trying.

He wore dark jeans, a black leather moto jacket over a gray tee, and a belt with a silver buckle. Ray-Bans were pushed up into his hair. It was an outfit in stark contrast to everyone else's athletic look, and it oozed unstoppable sex appeal. He looked like no one else in the room. The people around us watched as he reached the empty seat next to me and sat. Cell phones were discreetly aimed at us. The guy on the other side of Travis—a C-list celebrity who had won a reality show contest—introduced himself and took a selfie.

Travis complied, and then he turned to me.

Stay in character, Katie. Stay in character.

"Hi," I said politely.

He nodded. "Hi. I'm Travis."

"I'm Katie."

"Hi, Katie. Who's winning?"

He was following the script without a hitch. "Um, the Lakers are up by ten. But they've been fouling, so the Celtics are getting free throws. The coach just called a timeout."

"They've been fouling a lot this season," Travis said, sitting back in his chair to watch the action. "Or so I've seen on TV." He shot me a sideways look with a grin.

"That isn't your usual seat?" I asked. "I wouldn't know, because I've never been to a game before."

"Me neither. My friend gave me his ticket for tonight."

"Same here." I gave him a quick, shy smile before darting my gaze away.

We sat in silence for a few minutes as the game resumed and everyone's attention moved off of us. "You're late," I said to him under my breath, still watching the court.

"It worked, didn't it?" he shot back.

I pressed my lips together, because it killed me to admit—even to myself—that he'd made a bigger entrance than I'd planned. "You could have told me."

"Yeah," Travis agreed, his eyes on the game. "I could have."

I wiped my palms nervously on my thighs. According to the script, we were supposed to start talking, looking more and more engaged. Travis was supposed to make me laugh at least once. I hoped he'd make me truly laugh, because I didn't want to have to fake it. Fake laughing was one of the skills I needed to work on.

The halftime show ended and the third period started. Neither of us was talking. I kept my gaze ahead, wondering what Travis was doing. I couldn't tell from the corner of my eye. He seemed to be relaxed in his chair, watching the game. One of us had to talk, or this would all be over. Hadn't he paid attention to the script?

I would have to talk first. I was trying to come up with something believable to say when I felt Travis lean toward me, his shoulder pressing into mine. Suddenly I could smell leather and aftershave and male attraction, the scent sharp in my nose.

"Katie," Travis said close to my ear, "you're very fucking sexy."

I froze in shock.

This wasn't in the script. We were supposed to talk and laugh. He wasn't supposed to—

"Are you *coming on* to me?" I hissed.

"Yep." His breath touched my neck. "I think we should get naked. Preferably right after this game. Actually, let's not wait until it ends. Let's bail out right now."

I was hot all over in a flash, and I hated it. Travis White had just called me sexy. Was he acting? He had to be acting. Men didn't use that word for me. I was the nice girl, not the hot girl. Maybe he was confused and had forgotten his lines.

"We don't hook up yet," I said in a whisper, hoping to be helpful. "That's later."

His breath feathered over my neck again when he spoke, and I felt my skin flush hot. "Actually, it doesn't specify in the script when exactly we fuck. But you said you wanted to be bad for once. So I suggest tonight."

"Wait—for real?"

"I'm always for real."

I didn't know if he was confused or just messing with me, and suddenly I didn't care. "Travis," I said, just loud enough for him to hear and no one else. "Fuck off."

Travis leaned back and laughed. A real laugh, not offended

in the least. A few of the people around us turned, distracted.

I put a hand over my mouth. "Sorry."

Travis's laugh eased off. "Sorry? Why?"

I shook my head. The apology was a reflex, ingrained. Good girls always apologized when they were rude.

"Why not?" he asked good-naturedly. "Name one reason why we shouldn't hook up the first time we meet."

"We're supposed to talk first."

"Katie, we're talking right now."

I sighed. "Stop being obtuse."

"Stop being evasive. See, I can use big words, too."

I had no comeback for that. I just turned back to the game, fuming.

Travis waited me out, and even without looking at him, I could tell he was amused.

Finally, he said, "At least give me your number, Katie. It's inevitable. You wrote it into the scene."

"THAT WAS A DISASTER," I said on the phone to Stella later that night. "We need to call off the plan."

"I don't see why," Stella said. "You two met, you talked, you gave him your number. Everyone saw you at the game. What went so wrong?"

I was home in my apartment, where I had swathed myself in a bathrobe and curled up on my pretty cream-colored sofa in a position distressingly similar to fetal. Now that the night was over, it was hard to describe in words why Travis had made me so mad. "He was late," I said lamely. "Really late."

"That just means everyone noticed when he arrived."

I hated it when she was right. "He didn't charm me," I said. "He didn't make me laugh. He just...breathed in my ear."

"Katie, I've been divorced and trying to date in L.A. for four years. Trust me when I say that Travis White could breathe in *my* ear anytime."

"You know what I mean. He kept going off-script. We were supposed to talk and hit it off. There was no *spark*."

"What did he say to you?"

Even now, I couldn't repeat exactly what Travis had said, word for word. It felt strange to admit he'd called me sexy. He had to have been joking. "He suggested we change the script and hook up the first night we meet."

"So he tried to screw you?"

"*Fictionally*. Not in real life." Except that it *had* been real, according to him. Unless he was acting. This was already confusing.

"Hmm. Has he texted you yet?"

"No." The bottom dropped out of my stomach. "Wait. What if I get ghosted by my *fake* boyfriend? I'll never get over the humiliation."

"He isn't going to ghost you. I don't think."

"You don't *think*?"

"Well, he's Travis White. No one knows what he'll do. I'm checking his Instagram now—he didn't post about going to the game. He hasn't posted at all in six months."

I sank further into the sofa. This was the end. I was the terminal good girl, and instead of having a wild fling with the sexy bad boy, I'd get ghosted by him after telling him to fuck off, giving him my number, and waiting for him all night. I was the real life embodiment of a Taylor Swift song.

Stella could probably sense my spiral over the phone, because she said, "Don't panic, Katie. It really isn't—Oh."

I closed my eyes because I couldn't face the world anymore. "What does *oh* mean? Forget it, don't tell me. No one ever speak to me again."

"I searched Travis's name on Instagram and someone posted photos of you two at the game."

"What were we doing? Looking awkward? Because I think we just looked awkward, and that's why he'll never text me."

There was the chime of a text coming through on my phone. "Look at that," Stella said, her tone smug. "*No spark*, my ass."

Reluctantly, I took the phone from my ear and tapped her text message. Then I stared in disbelief.

Someone had taken shots of us from across the court, zoomed in. *Saw Travis White at the Lakers game tonight*, the caption said. *I don't know who she is, but I think he's smitten.*

The first one was of Travis laughing. I had my hand over my mouth. It was after I'd told him off. It didn't look awkward. It looked, in fact, *exactly* like we were hitting it off.

In the second photo, we weren't talking. I was staring at the game in what I believed was an awkward moment. My expression was rapt—thank you, acting training—but my posture was tense, and my hands were on my thighs because I was quietly wiping my palms.

Still, I was obviously watching the game. But Travis wasn't. Travis was looking at me.

He was relaxed in his seat, but his head was turned, his blue gaze fixed on my profile. He was stunningly gorgeous, and he was ignoring the game completely, as if he couldn't look away.

From me.

I put the phone back to my ear in shock. "What the hell is that?" I asked Stella.

"*That* is spark," was the reply. "The kind you can't buy. Jimson Greer can eat my ass, because we don't need him. We have Travis."

I pulled the phone away and stared at the photos again. I

stared at them so long that I had to put Stella on speaker so I wouldn't have to stop looking. Travis and I didn't look like two strangers bickering about my script. In these photos, we looked like we had instant chemistry.

"Are you seeing your Instagram?" Stella asked.

I had turned off my Instagram notifications years ago, because even though it was nice that a lot of my fans followed me, it was too much to get notifications all day, some of which were mean or upsetting. I didn't need my phone notifying me at three in the morning that someone thought I was fat.

So I had given Gwen, my part-time assistant, access to all of my social media in case there was something I needed to be alerted to. Like now.

As if on cue, a text came in from Gwen. *Check your IG. It's poppin!* Gwen was younger than me, and her texts regularly made me feel ancient.

I opened Instagram and stared at the notifications clicking in. People identifying me in the photo and tagging me. People resharing the photo. People posting their own photos and tagging me.

"It won't go viral," Stella said on the speaker. "We're not there yet, but this is just the first meeting. It looks good. Stick to the plan, Katie. I promise you it will work."

After we hung up, I closed Instagram and stared at the photos again. I couldn't get over Travis's expression as he looked at me. How had I not noticed it? How was he that good of an actor? Because he had to be acting. Yet the look on his face was so convincing. Did he—

My phone chimed with a text from an unknown number, and I immediately knew it was him.

I'm leaving L.A. tonight. Want to come with me?

SIX

Travis

SHE CALLED JUST after I had popped the trunk of my Camaro in Andy's driveway and was hauling my suitcase into it.

I knew before I looked at the screen that it was Katie. I had already talked to everyone else I needed to talk to. After the game, I got a single thumbs-up emoji text from Jonathan—his review of my performance, which raised him in my estimation. The less my agent talked to me, the better.

"Hey, Katie," I said when I answered. "If you want me to pick you up, give me your address."

"Travis." She was steamed, but she was trying to be polite. It was cute. "What does this mean, you're leaving L.A.?"

I slammed the trunk of the Camaro closed. Andy's driveway was dark, his street empty this late. I'd said goodbye to Andy already and promised to let him know when I got where I was going. A sprinkler turned on a few houses down, the shushing sound cool in the night air.

"It means I'm leaving."

"For where?"

"No idea. Want to come?"

"What are you talking about? We're supposed to go on a date in a few days. At Nobu."

I ran my hand along my Camaro. I hadn't driven much in the last six months, and I fucking loved this car. "Katie, come on. Forget the script. Pack your bag and I'll pick you up. We'll hit the road and have fun."

"What is this?" She sounded outraged, and—worse—almost hurt. "Are you screwing up the plan on purpose? Why? Is it a joke? Are you making fun of me?"

"I'm not making fun of you. Jesus." I shook my head. "You want to ditch being a good girl for a while. You want to have a wild time with a bad boy. This is how you do it. You do something impulsive and risky and yeah, maybe stupid. That's the risk. That's the *fun*."

"You just said you don't know where you're going. I don't even know you."

"But we hit it off. You've seen the pictures, haven't you? Of course you have. Katie, we hit it *off*."

There was a pause on the other end of the line. "The pictures are good," she admitted. "That doesn't mean I'd drop everything for a man I don't know. I want to be bad, not crazy."

"Here's my version of the story," I said. "We meet at the game, and I think you're the hottest fucking woman I've ever seen. I take my shot, because of course I do, but you don't go for it. You're too good for me, and we both know it."

"Travis."

"But you like me," I continued. "You give me your number because you think I'm hot as fuck and you want to see me again. You can't stop thinking about me, even though you know you shouldn't. You're having fantasies about me, and some of them are so filthy—"

"Got it," she interrupted. "Skip ahead, please."

"So I call you, and I tell you I think you're hot as fuck, too. Meeting you has made me realize I've been sleepwalking. I want more. I want to feel alive again, and in order to do that, I have to get out of this city. I want to forget everything for a while and just drive with a beautiful woman in the car with me. I think that beautiful woman should be you. And—because you think I'm hot as fuck—you do it. You pack your bags and go."

She hadn't hung up on me yet. I called that a win. "What do we do on this hypothetical trip?" she asked, and I stopped myself from pumping my fist. She was intrigued.

"We sightsee," I told her. "We go wherever we want. We eat great food. We talk. We catch some good music or some good movies. We have nonstop incredible sex."

"Travis!"

"Okay, I know that part is fictional. We can play Scrabble in our hotel room. I'm not trying to fuck you." There was a second of silence on the line, because this was an absolute lie. "Well, I *am* trying to fuck you, but I'm a gentleman, so it's cool."

Surprisingly, my mummified dick *was* trying to get into a woman for the first time in an excruciatingly long time. But he could wait. I'd probably have to watch some porn just to remember how sex worked. Maybe I'd need diagrams.

"I can't," Katie said, and though she sounded sure, she probably didn't know that she also sounded sad about it. "I have a life here, an apartment. I just finished shooting a movie, and there's promo to do, and… I can't drop everything after meeting a guy once. It just isn't me."

"You wanted sexy and unpredictable and hot." I quoted

what she'd said in our first meeting. "This is the last thing anyone thinks you'll do. Which is exactly what you're looking for."

"And what happens after we take this little trip? The plan was for us to have a relationship, not a fling."

"After the trip, we have a relationship," I said. "In fact, I think we should shack up."

"Excuse me? Absolutely not. Didn't you even *read* the script?"

"I read it."

She sounded sad again. "Travis, I appreciate that you're trying, I really do. But I'm sticking to the script, or I'm not doing this at all."

Surprisingly, that hurt. I spent a second feeling the thump of pain deep in my gut, because I'd been hoping she'd say yes. I hadn't hoped for anything in a long time.

But she wasn't saying yes. And that stung more than I had thought it would.

"You have my number," I managed to say after a second. "Call it anytime. I mean anytime."

"Good luck, Travis."

"Good luck, Katie."

There was nothing else to say.

I WAS FLYING ON IMPULSE. I had done it a hundred times onstage, where I could wing it based on what the crowd wanted from me, but I hadn't had room to be impulsive in my personal life in a long time. Not until I lost everything and no one gave a shit what I did anymore.

I'd once had tens of thousands of fans, a staff, and an

entourage of hangers-on. Now I drove out of this bitch of a city with no one to see me off.

I decided to drive north. I put the music on loud and tried to put the image of Katie Armstrong behind me. She wasn't the first person who didn't want me, and she wouldn't be the last.

Sometime around two in the morning, I stopped at an all-night truck stop. I wasn't sleepy yet, so I bought a syrupy fountain Coke and brought it back to my car. I picked up my phone and took a selfie, leaning against my car with the truck stop sign behind me lit up against the night sky. I uploaded the photo to Instagram and wrote a caption: *I'm off to new adventures. Love you all.* Then I hit Post.

I had 3.2 million followers, and I hadn't posted in six months.

I tossed the phone on the passenger seat, started the car, and went back to the long drive north, wondering if I'd ever get tired.

SEVEN

Katie

I HAD FIVE EXCELLENT, very productive days.
 I cleaned my rented L.A. apartment, dusting off the plastic plants and wiping down the frosty-white kitchen. This place had come furnished, which had worked for me because when I rented it I'd had the idea that L.A. would be just one place I'd spend my time, only when I was shooting here. Aside from going home to my parents in Minnesota, I had planned to also spend time being an artsy bohemian in New York, and maybe jetting to London to do theater from time to time. I was a working actress—I could go anywhere, be anything.
 The reality was that except for occasional location shoots in glamorous places like Calgary or a back lot in Orange County, I lived in L.A. all the time, which meant this rented apartment with its rented furniture was it. Everything in here was white and cream, which looked great in photos but made me feel weird, as if I wasn't supposed to touch anything or actually sit

my ass on any of the furniture. The doorman downstairs had taken days off last week for his nose job, and a woman on the floor below me had offered to personally give me an herbal colonic. It was home, but it wasn't exactly homey.

Still, I tidied it and did my laundry. I worked out every day, even though I wasn't prepping for a role. I drank nutrient-rich smoothies. I deep conditioned my hair. I did a quarterly review of my finances with my accountant. I did a five-step skin routine before bed. I was *on it*.

And once in bed in my bright-white bedroom every night, I pulled up the picture Travis had posted on his Instagram and stared at it.

Leaning against his Camaro in the middle of the night, Coke in hand. I could see the snake tattoo winding around his bare arm, because he'd taken the leather jacket off. Even in the unforgiving light of the truck stop sign, he was a gorgeous man. Those blue eyes. The shadow of late-night stubble on his jaw. The crinkles just visible at the corners of his eyes. *I'm off to new adventures. Love you all.*

His followers had gone crazy for it. It had taken them no time at all to figure out that the truck stop in the photo was a few hours north of L.A. Aside from the bots and weirdos in the comment section, there were also true fans who hoped he was all right, who wanted to know where he was going, who wanted him to make new music. They wondered where he'd been. They'd worried that in the storm that had been his life for the last while, they'd somehow lost him. They wanted him back.

The more I looked at the photo, the more I understood the sentiment.

Lying in my crisp sheets, wearing my favorite pajamas, I mooned over him silently like a teenaged girl. I had been ditched by my fake boyfriend.

Except I hadn't really been ditched, had I? He'd invited me

to come with him, and he'd meant it. He'd wanted to be at that truck stop with me, and the reason he was alone was because I'd said no.

Stella had been livid at Travis's desertion, but only briefly. Like the pro she was, she had assured me that she would come up with a list of alternate candidates. The boyfriend idea was a good one, she maintained. Edgar Pinsent was in Romania reworking his script, and no one would ever know that Travis White hadn't worked out. We'd find someone else, she said, and I would get the part if it killed her.

She'd also sent me another script that had come across her desk. A limited series—five episodes. It was about a divorced single mom who moves home to Montana to nurse her sick dad and finds love on a ranch. *It's got heart!* Stella wrote to me. *It's mature. It could be a great change of direction.*

I didn't read it. I didn't have to. I already knew how it ended.

On the fifth night, I did what I swore I wouldn't. I was only human, and humans can only take so much. So I caved.

I opened TikTok, where I had a secret account under a fake name, and looked up KatieWatch.

KatieWatch was an account run by one of my fans. People sent her photos and videos of me—at appearances, on the set, or just going about my life—and KatieWatch posted them. The account only had fifteen hundred followers, because a) being a superfan of mine was extremely niche, and b) I didn't lead an interesting life. Hence the Travis White idea.

Still, KatieWatch existed, which meant I had to spend every day *not* looking at it. If you've never had a TikTok account—even a small one—dedicated to you, then you have no idea how hard that is. Celebrities, they're just like us! They want to know what people are saying about them, and whether someone got an unflattering photo that gave them a double chin, and whether they said something that made them look like an asshole.

So I caved, and I peeked at KatieWatch. I didn't see a double chin, or me being an asshole. I saw Travis.

KatieWatch had not missed our meetup at the Lakers game. The top video on the page was taken from across the court. Travis looked at me, and then he leaned in and spoke in my ear. A brief exchange, and then I told him to fuck off—you could read the words clearly on my lips. Travis laughed, and I put my hand over my mouth.

The video had over three hundred thousand views. I tapped the comments.

Excuse me?? Katie with Travis White?? I love it.

My god, he's hot.

I wouldn't picture them together, but he's kind of perfect for her?

Oh yes, girl, get it.

The way he looks at her!

She hasn't dated anyone in so long. She deserves some fun!

What did he say to her? I'm dying to know.

Are they actually dating? Does anyone know?

I think if Travis White sat next to me I would actually expire.

Okay, this NEEDS to happen. I need some vicarious romance in my life!

Wow, they look SO GOOD.

The last one was right. We *did* look good. Not just Travis—damn how beautiful he was—but me, too. When I looked at the video of us, I *liked* how I looked. Even in jeans and a T-shirt, I looked pretty and relaxed and sexy. I looked like a woman who would get hit on by a world famous rock star and casually tell him to fuck off. I looked at the woman in the video, and I thought she was hot. I liked her.

I wanted to be her.

Which was weird, because I *was* her. But I wanted to be her all the time.

I closed TikTok, but not before noticing that the Katie-Watch account didn't have fifteen hundred followers anymore. It now had three thousand. It had doubled in the last five days.

I put my phone down and lay back in bed, staring at the ceiling. The silence pressed down on me.

After a million years, I fell asleep.

THE NEXT MORNING, Stella sent a list of Travis's replacements.

I scrolled through the names on my laptop at my kitchen table while I drank my morning coffee with oat milk. I had no idea why I put oat milk in my coffee, except that dairy was bad for some reason and almond milk was environmentally wasteful. Or was that cashew milk? I didn't think there was a problem with oat milk, except that it made my coffee taste like someone had wet a piece of old newspaper and placed it into my drink.

A reality show guy. A guy who had gone viral with a hot TikTok dance. An actor I had co-starred with a few years ago—*We could play up that you didn't date back then but never forgot each other*, Stella wrote. I didn't remember much about him except that before we shot our kissing scene, he'd said "Let's get to it" as if we were about to sand a hardwood floor.

I pushed my kitchen chair back and stood. I left my awful oat milk on the table and walked into the bedroom.

I took my suitcase from my closet, put it on the bed, and opened it. I started to put clothes into it.

I did not think about this. My hands worked of their own

accord. I felt no emotion at all. I had no plan. I simply kept packing.

When I had finished with clothes and had moved on to toiletries, I picked up my phone. I scrolled past Stella's texts, asking me what I thought of the alternate boyfriends, of the Montana ranch script. I scrolled to Travis's number and dialled it. I didn't care that it was early in the morning and he might not be awake. I assumed that rock stars slept late. It didn't matter.

"Hey, Katie," he said when he answered. He didn't sound annoyed or sleepy. He sounded pleased.

I ignored the shiver his voice gave me, which turned my knees to jelly. "Hello, Travis," I said, polite because I was born in Minnesota and politeness was drilled into my bones. "Where are you?"

"Portland."

Portland, I thought. I could work with that. "Are you just passing through?"

"Nah, I decided to stay here a while. The road trip was fun, but not as fun alone."

I dropped my makeup bag into my suitcase, then my phone charger. "Do you have somewhere to stay?"

"I got an apartment."

"How did you get an apartment so fast?" I closed my eyes. "Wait, don't answer that." This was supposed to be impulsive. I really needed to stop dwelling on details.

There was amusement in Travis's voice. "Okay, I won't answer. Are you asking because you're changing your mind?"

I was being impulsive, but still—he was a rock star, and I needed the smallest bit of self respect. "I just have one question," I said to him. "Are you seeing anyone else? Tell me the truth. This won't work if you're sleeping around."

He was silent for a second, and then he laughed.

I stood frowning. I wasn't trying to be funny.

"I'm not seeing anyone," Travis said when his laughter died down. "I cannot express to you how deeply, how profoundly I am not seeing anyone at all."

"Not even physically?"

"My body is a temple," Travis said. "I could ascend to heaven and be judged pure by the angels. Even my right hand has taken a vacation."

I winced. "I didn't need quite that much detail, but okay."

"Come to Portland, Katie," he said in that smoky, sexy voice of his. "I'm asking you. Let's make this fun."

Damn it. *Damn* it.

I slapped my suitcase shut.

"Send me the address," I said. "I'll be there today."

He sent it. And when I left, I took my laptop, but I left my oat milk coffee where it was.

EIGHT

Travis

WHAT WAS I DOING? Not long ago, I was a semi-sentient head placed atop a body made of clay. A houseplant. Then Katie Armstrong had showed up—she had literally been delivered to my house and offered to me. A beautiful, smart, sexy way out of my problems. And instead of following her script, I'd left town.

Travis White, fucking genius, right here.

I was bad at following rules, even when it fucked me over. As a kid, I had skipped school to rehearse with my shitty teenage band, then cheated on tests to barely pass my classes. I had used fake ID's to play shows before I was twenty-one. I had gone on tour with my shitty teenage band instead of getting a summer job as a camp counselor, which would have earned some actual money. My bandmates and I had driven off in an old van, sure that we were destined for great adventures and stardom at eighteen.

We'd lasted exactly sixteen days before my bandmates decided they hated road life and wanted to go home. Talk about useless. I'd wanted to keep going—I was barely winded. But we'd gone home and broken up.

That same summer, after my failed tour, the Road Kings came to Baltimore, my hometown. I went to the show—using my fake ID—and it blew my mind.

The Road Kings were a legendary touring band by then. They'd never had a chart hit, but anyone who was anyone in the music scene never missed a Road Kings show. They'd played an old theater that had seen better days. The tickets were cheap, the beer was cheaper, the crowd was rowdy, and the band had blown the roof off. They were in their twenties, but they'd been playing together for years, and it showed. They were tight. They were talented. The songs were good. Their lead singer was Denver Gilchrist—skinny, dark-haired, good-looking, with a voice that could growl or scream or make you weep. Onstage, he was fucking incandescent, as if he was lit up from within. He'd raise his arms and the crowd would jump as one, howling the words along with him. It was religious. It was the best musical experience I'd ever had.

It was exactly what I'd dreamed of doing if my bandmates hadn't chickened out. I decided two things that night. One, I'd get another band. And two, no matter how good they were, I hated the Road Kings.

I joined another shitty band, and then another. Most bands don't work, just like most dating relationships don't work. People don't click, or they go their separate ways. You get ghosted, and then you ghost someone else. I struck out until a producer noticed me. He knew a manager, who knew other musicians and record execs. I got thrown into a session with four guys I didn't know, and we were given songs someone else had written. We were paid to rehearse and jam for a week, during which we cut demos of the songs. The demos were given to record execs, and suddenly we were a band called Seven Dog Down.

I cut a record with those four guys I barely knew, and the first single hit number one. I was twenty years old.

In all of the madness that followed, I knew now that I should have seen the signs. When someone comes to you, it's never because it benefits you. It's only because it benefits them. Those producers, managers, and execs looked at us and saw a way to make money.

From day one, we were worked like dogs—tours, rehearsals, videos, photo shoots, promo, press tours. People loved the music, and we were famous, so what was there to complain about? It was a great life. Except that we were all taking whatever we had to in order to keep up the schedule, and at the end of the day we somehow didn't have much money in our bank accounts. There are a lot of expenses, we were told. They have to be paid up front. Eventually, the profits would roll in.

So we kept going. My bandmates and I barely talked, and what started out as a coworking relationship turned to mutual hate. We were exhausted. I was pretty sure at least two of us were full-blown addicts, or almost there. Our drummer got married and divorced twice and our bass player got a married actress pregnant. Our lead guitar was such a narcissistic asshole I wanted to kick his teeth in every time I looked at him. Eventually he got a lawyer and filed a suit that claimed that he was "the essence of Seven Dog Down" and should be entitled to most of the money.

That's when the shit hit the fan.

More lawsuits. We didn't have much money, it turned out, because management had kept most of it. We didn't have rights to the band name or any of the songs, because we hadn't written them. The record deals fucked us over at every turn.

We could have fought it better if we stuck together, but we hated each other, so we sued each other instead. Everything was still in the courts, except for the trickle of money that was what I was actually owed under those shitty contracts I'd signed.

So I was understandably pissed when my best friend, Finn Wiley, said, "I think you should work with the Road Kings."

I was staying at Finn's house outside of Seattle. My road trip had led me here, probably because I was skilled at mooching off of people, especially my friends. Finn didn't seem to mind. His house was big. He'd had a huge hit song when he was sixteen, one of those songs that you couldn't escape for an entire summer. The albums after that one had bombed, so Finn left the music business and lived off his royalties and investments like a sane person who had signed decent contracts and now had money coming in. I could never hate him, partly because he let me sponge shamelessly off of him and partly because he was the best guy I knew.

"Fuck off," I told him.

I was lying on the floor of his music room, which was his basement. It was my favorite room of his house—an open space filled with instruments, amps, mics, speakers, and a killer recording and mixing setup. Finn made music down here. I was lying on the floor because I was busy loving up Finn's old dog, Gary. I rubbed Gary's head, his ears, his chest, and his grizzled face as I told off one of the only friends I had left.

"I've never understood why you hate the Road Kings so much," Finn said.

"Easy. Because they're dicks."

"But you're also a dick," he pointed out. "I don't see the problem."

I kissed the top of Gary's head shamelessly, and his tail

thumped the floor in bliss. This dog didn't think I was a dick, or a failure. This dog thought I was the greatest thing on earth.

"You don't even know them," Finn continued. "Not really. Have you ever even met them?"

"Denver Gilchrist said onstage at a show that we sucked," I said.

"Yes. And you retaliated by sending them a bottle of champagne that was actually a glitter bomb. They opened it backstage right before a show."

I smiled an evil smile. The glitter champagne had been my idea. I knew that the Road Kings' drummer, Axel de Vries, was sober, so I had made sure that the fake champagne was labeled non-alcoholic. That was how dedicated I was to making sure those guys would open it and play a show covered in glitter.

"The rivalry is stupid," Finn said. He was sprawled on the sofa, wearing basketball shorts and an old tee. He ran a hand through his tousled brown hair. In his thirties, Finn still had the remnants of his teenage-dream good looks—not just the face, but the way he simply never looked bad. He *looked* like a decent guy, which was what he was. He could sing, play multiple instruments, write songs, produce, mix—anything. He was even a great dancer, due to his dance training as a kid. Finn had had rough times in life, but I didn't think he'd ever been called a houseplant.

"Who cares if it's stupid?" I said. "I'm not working with them. And I'm sure they don't want to work with me, either."

Finn shook his head. His fiancée, Juliet Barstow, played bass with the Road Kings. She'd started as a fill-in when their bass player took leave, but even after he came back, Juliet stayed in the band. "I don't think that's true. I think they'd work with you. In fact, I think it would be perfect."

I rolled my eyes. Gary's tail thumped, and I rubbed his ears again. "Do tell."

"They built their own studio and started their own record company. They release their music independently now, and they're more successful than ever."

"Gee, good for them. What does that have to do with me?"

"Well, they make money now," Finn said, his gaze locking with mine. "Good money. That they, you know, keep."

My hand scratching Gary's ear slowed. There had been years and years when I didn't think about money—it never crossed my mind. Flights were booked, hotel rooms were ready, cars whisked us around from one show to another. For Seven Dog Down, money seemed to simply happen, the way oxygen and breathing happened. It was everywhere, so I never thought about it.

I thought about money now. I'd unloaded all the dumb, thoughtless things I'd bought when I was famous—homes, cars—and I still had very little to live on. My money, so plentiful, had vanished into a black hole of legal fees I didn't fully understand. I had my Camaro, a few belongings, and that was it.

I didn't need much, but I needed something. I couldn't mooch off friends forever. I was a good-looking, stupid guy in his thirties, who had cheated to graduate high school and had lived his entire twenties with his head up his ass. I wasn't exactly employable.

If I tried, I could probably get my agent to find me a paying gig. Acting, or maybe modeling. He could land me on a reality show or find me a ghostwriter to write my memoir. I could live the has-been life. But I really only knew how to do one thing: make music.

What if I...made new music? My own music? And it made money?

As incredible as it sounded, I had never once seriously considered this in the last year and a half. I had been part of Seven Dog Down for so long that it felt ingrained in my identity. We'd been handed songs to play. It had all been so easy. Unfulfilling, sure. But easy.

I hadn't written any songs in years. But what if I started?

The deal with Katie Armstrong was supposed to be part of reviving my career. Andy and Jonathan were pushing me to do something other than sit around. But even though I'd thoroughly fucked that deal up, a faint signal had gotten through my skull and penetrated my brain. I was young, healthy, sober, and very much not dead. I could do something.

I narrowed my eyes at Finn. "What's the difference between working for the Road Kings and working for the record companies that already fucked me over?"

Finn smiled, because he knew he'd pulled me in. "The difference is that the Road Kings don't fuck anyone over. Do you think I'd work with anyone who would do that? Would Juliet?"

I stroked Gary's head and thought about it. No one knew the music business better than Finn, who had started when he was a kid. And Juliet was a lifelong musician. She'd seen every trick to screw over musicians, and then some. The music business is still a boys' club, which means that no matter how hard I'd been screwed over, a woman had been screwed over ten times harder.

As if she'd been summoned by a dark spell, Juliet came down the stairs. She wore vintage jeans with flowers stitched on the pockets and a one-shoulder shirt with the words *Just Try Me* on the front. Her shoulder-length blond hair was tied partly up, and she wore dark eyeliner. "I'm going to the studio," she said to Finn, ignoring me. "I'll give you some alone time with your boyfriend."

"You mean Gary's boyfriend," Finn corrected her.

Juliet looked at me, and I hugged Gary harder.

"I like your dog," I said to her.

"I know."

I had been friends with Finn long before Juliet arrived in his life, and that was the only reason she tolerated me. So far, I couldn't charm her, make her laugh, or otherwise win her over, but I still tried. I gave her my most killer smile, but she only rolled her eyes.

She walked back to Finn, bent over him, and kissed him soundly. "I'll see you at the studio later," he promised her. Then she was gone.

"Your girlfriend is hot," I said to Finn.

"I heard that," she shouted from the top of the stairs. "Keep your eyes to yourself. Also, thank you."

"You're welcome," I shouted up the stairs.

"She is," Finn agreed. He had the look on his face he always had when she was around. He was crazy in love with her. It was interesting to observe. I had had girlfriends, but I had never had that look on my face in my life. I was sure of it.

For a second, I wondered what it felt like. To love a woman like that. To have her love you back. How did you get anyone to love you back?

I couldn't stay here anymore. Finn and I had had lots of fun as single guys, but he wasn't a single guy anymore. I was in the way.

So, as usual, I said something impulsive that I couldn't take back. "If I'm going to work in Portland, I'll need somewhere to stay."

Finn looked surprised. "You'll do it?"

I shrugged. "If those fuckfaces are willing to work with me, I guess I'll do it. I need some time to write first. Do you know where I can get a good apartment?"

"Sure I do," Finn said. "You can use mine."

I stared at him. "You have an apartment?"

He nodded. "The studio is in Vancouver, and the commute

from here is too long for us to do all the time. We had to leave Gary alone too much. So we got a place in Portland to use when we have to be at the studio a lot. We bring Gary so he isn't home alone."

"But you're here now, at the house."

"Because it's quiet now. We aren't in the middle of a big project. We prefer being here when we can, and Gary prefers it, too. The apartment is empty. You're welcome to use it."

I looked away from him, turning my gaze back to the dog. People were too nice to me. First Andy, and now Finn. "I'll pay you rent," I managed as my throat tried to close.

"Don't pay me rent," Finn said gently. "It's sitting empty, honestly. It's fine." When I didn't speak, he continued. "Do you remember when you stayed with me in Paris? Years ago?"

"I remember." Finn's third album had tanked, and he'd quit the music business. On a break between tours, I'd stayed with him in a small flat in Paris. We'd had a few months of fun, drinking and clubbing and trying to get laid.

"You remember what I was like then?" Finn asked. "I was lost and depressed. Aimless. I wasn't myself. You showed up, Travis, and you stayed. You didn't judge and you didn't try to fix me. You just stuck with me and pulled me out of it. You were my best friend, and you still are. Just last year, you told me to release my music and get back in the game, and you were right. It changed my life when I did that. So, no. Don't pay me rent."

I sighed. It was nice of him to bring that shit up. But one of these days, I would have to be a grownup.

Today, apparently, was not that day.

"I'll take the apartment," I said. "Give me the address."

IT WAS A NICE APARTMENT. It was on the eighth floor of a century-old warehouse that had been remodeled into loft apartments for hipsters. There was an indie coffee shop on the street level. I did not have the luxury of scoffing at the Portland man-bun Birkenstock pretentiousness of it, because not only was the place free, it was also kind of awesome.

There was a couch and a big TV in the main room, a kitchen with stainless steel appliances and a big countertop, and a bathroom with a huge walk-in shower. In the middle of the main room, an open staircase wound up to the loft area, which held a big bed, two dressers, and a closet. The floor-to-ceiling windows looked out on the city. Yeah, I would wear Birkenstocks if it meant I could live here. Maybe I should buy a pair.

The day was gloomy, with lowering rain clouds. I made my way up the staircase—noting that the stairs would be impossible while drunk—and dropped my bags next to the bed. I lay on top of the covers, thinking that I would just test the mattress to see if I liked it. Seconds later, I was asleep.

I awoke to my phone ringing on the bedside table. The gloom outside the windows was exactly the same as it had been when I closed my eyes. Had I been asleep for fifteen minutes or fifteen hours? Could be anything. If it had been a brief nap, it had hit me like a bulldozer, because I felt like I'd been here for years. Groggily, I reached for the phone. Then I sat up, jerking off the pillow and swinging my legs down so fast my feet slapped the floor. "Fuck," I said out loud.

Katie was calling.

"Be cool, man, be cool." I said it aloud to the empty apartment. I straightened my shoulders, loosened my jaw. Then I answered the call.

"Hey, Katie." My voice sounded normal. I thought.

"Hello, Travis. Where are you?"

Just the sound of her voice, so calm and polite and pretty—my pulse sped up. I rolled my shoulders. With one simple phone greeting, I suddenly knew I wanted her here with me. I needed to convince her. She had to be calling me to give me a chance, and I had to take it.

It turned out her biggest reservation was that I might be screwing someone else, which struck me as funny. I was alone in this apartment with no idea what I was doing, and—I glanced at the time—I had just slept for fifteen hours, because it was *the next morning*. The best cuddle I'd had in years was with Finn's dog. It was safe to say that I was no longer living the rock star life.

Katie seemed to take my word for it. Then she said she was coming. Today.

I played it cool, only because it took a moment for the words to sink in. After we'd said goodbye and hung up, I stared at the wall.

I had asked Katie to drop everything and come here to pretend to have an affair. And she had said...yes?

She had said she was coming *today*.

"Holy shit," I whispered, and then I got up and bolted for the shower.

NINE

Katie

THE WOMAN next to me on the plane was around sixty. She wore a soft gray cardigan over a cotton shirt, and pinned to the cardigan was a flower brooch. She gave me a polite look that said *please don't talk to me,* and then she faced forward and didn't look at me again.

Not talking was fine with me. Still, I made up a story for the woman in my head. I decided that her name was Mrs. Cooper, and she had retired from a long career as a high school guidance counselor. Her husband had retired too, and he was driving her nuts around the house, so she was taking a trip to see her sister in Portland. Mrs. Cooper was wise and gave great advice, and if I told her what I was doing, she would probably tell me to turn around and go home.

I couldn't do that once we had taken off, so I scarfed six pretzels the size of my thumbnail and second guessed my life choices.

My confidence had fled. This was stupid. I barely knew Travis White, and he was probably a jerk. I should find a real boyfriend instead of going to all the trouble of setting up a fake one. What was wrong with a real man, one who would take me on dates? I could find one of those. I had done it before, and I could do it again. Everything about this was crazy. No one was going to notice if I was fake dating Travis White, and Edgar Pinsent wouldn't care. I should tell Stella I'd take the mom role. I'd take the role with the shirtless plumber. Everything had been going just fine. Why had I thought I should upend my career? What had I been thinking?

It got dark outside the window, even though it was noon. The seat belt light went on, and the captain made an announcement that was incomprehensible except for the words *storm* and *a little turbulence*. As if on cue, the plane jerked.

No big deal. It was a short flight—just over two hours. What could go wrong on a flight this short?

Forty-five minutes later, I was gripping the arms of my seat with white-knuckled, sweaty hands as the plane jerked harder and harder. The flight crew were pasty-faced, kids were crying, and at least one person near the back was definitely throwing up. Next to me, Mrs. Cooper was crouched in her seat with her hands up as if she expected us to drop from the sky. I thought she might be right.

I thought about my parents. My friends. Stella, whose texts I hadn't answered before we took off. I thought of *High School Reunion*, which would be the last film I made if I died right now. Netflix would release it with a special dedication to me in the opening credits. People would shake their heads and say it was sad. My fan pages would mourn. KatieWatch would have to shut down.

If I died right now, that would be my mark on the world— Netflix romcoms. I would never have made something really,

really good. I would never have made something that challenged me.

I would never have been sexy and unpredictable and hot. I would never have kissed the bad boy rock star with the gorgeous blue eyes. I would never have done *anything* fun.

"Oh, dear Jesus," Mrs. Cooper said as the plane jerked again. Her cheeks were wet. She was crying.

I was going to die here on this flight with strangers. I wasn't going to go peacefully in my deathbed fifty years from now, full of great memories of sleeping bag sex with Travis White.

It was the last thought I had before we dropped like a roller coaster and everyone screamed.

TWO HOURS LATER, I knocked on Travis's apartment door. I was wet from the thunderstorm still happening outside. My knees were rubbery, and I was lightheaded. I remembered almost nothing about getting here from the airport, about the concierge letting me up because Travis had given him my name. I was still shaky, and my skin was clammy.

The door swung open. Travis was wearing a long-sleeved T-shirt and dark gray sweatpants, and even though he was no longer poolside in California, he still looked golden. His hair was clean and tousled. His eyes were vivid blue. He wore a thin silver chain that disappeared into the neckline of his shirt. He smiled like he was happy to see me, and the sight was so beautiful it made me crazy.

I let go of the handle of my roller suitcase, and before Travis could speak, I stepped forward, put my arms around his neck, and kissed him.

He hesitated for only the briefest second, and then he kissed me back. His arms came around my waist, and he pulled me to him and leaned in. He shifted his weight to one foot, and I heard the apartment door bang shut behind me as he kicked it closed.

Then I was kissing Travis White, and it was even better than I had thought it would be.

He tasted decadent and satisfying, like a buttery pastry. His skin was warm, his mouth expert as it explored mine. He teased my lips apart, then relished me like I was a gourmet meal, his palms sliding up my back. He smelled like soap and a primal man-smell that made me feral. I kissed him with everything I had, my body fused to his, my arms wound around him, my hands in his hair. My brain shut down as I soaked him in, and the only thing I knew was that I wanted what I wanted, and I wanted it now.

When the kiss finally broke with the slow cooling of a glacier melting, Travis's skin was flushed and his pupils were dark. He didn't let me go.

"Hi," he rasped.

"Hi," I whispered. I didn't let him go, either. We stared at each other for a long second.

"That was quite a greeting," Travis said.

It occurred to me, dimly, that I might be giving him the wrong idea. I had showed up on his doorstep and flung myself at him. I should probably do something to get some distance, appear more businesslike.

I cleared my throat. "I, um, thought we should probably kiss. You know, for the script."

"Yeah?" he said.

God, he smelled so good. Why were my arms still around his neck? I would remove them any minute now. "Yes. If we're going to give the impression that we're...doing things, then we should be...comfortable with each other, by which I mean—oh, my God, Travis."

He had dipped his head and was kissing the side of my neck, trailing his lips over my skin. I felt that touch all the way down my body. Even my shoulders and the backs of my legs were tingling. It was incredible.

He lifted his lips from my neck and rumbled his sexy voice in my ear. "It's a good idea. For the script." Then he lowered his mouth again, tasting my skin.

I tried to keep focus as he made my body light up. "It needs to be believable," I managed. "It isn't believable if we look like we barely know each other. Body language, and all that. We want to sell the relationship."

"You taste like vanilla," Travis said. "I don't know how that's possible."

"Also, I almost died on the flight here," I said.

He lifted his head and frowned in concern. "What? Are you all right?"

I let out a breath. "I'm fine, except that I'm going to make sure my will is up to date. Okay, maybe it wasn't actually that close to death. But it felt like it. The turbulence was so bad even Mrs. Cooper couldn't handle it, and she was a high school guidance counselor."

He looked confused, and I didn't blame him. "Well, I'm glad you're okay. Are you hungry? I stocked the kitchen. You probably want to freshen up. Oh, and I want to show you something. Be right back."

He let me go, and just like that, he was heading up the staircase to the upstairs bedroom. Sobriety hit me, and I realized several things at the same time.

First, I was disappointed that Travis wasn't touching me anymore.

Second, I was hungry and I needed to pee.

And third, I wasn't embarrassed about jumping Travis. At all.

I waited for the anxiety to hit, waited for my brain to start second- and third-guessing what I had just done. Waited for the certainty that it was crazy, that I didn't know Travis, that I should apologize, that I needed to take control of the situation and set it right. And I didn't feel…any of it.

I didn't feel weird that I was staying here with him. In fact, now that I looked around, it was a nice place. I went to the bathroom and washed up, and when I came out, Travis had pulled a chair up to the bar-height kitchen island. In front of him was a cheap spiral notebook and a pen.

"Okay?" he asked me.

"Yeah." I opened the fridge—which was indeed stocked—and took out a bottled fruit smoothie. "How did you get this place?" I asked as I looked for a glass.

Travis flipped open his notebook. "I borrowed it from Finn Wiley."

I put the bottle down in shock. "Finn *Wiley*? As in, 'Ice Cream Girlfriend' Finn Wiley?"

Travis rolled his eyes at my mention of the huge hit song from years ago. "That's him."

"I love that song. I listen to it on repeat sometimes when I need to get in a mood for a scene. He's a friend of yours?"

Travis shrugged, as if this was unimportant. His friends included Andy Rockweller and Finn Wiley, and it wasn't a big deal to him. I'd met many celebrities—or I'd been in their orbit at parties, which counted as the same thing—but I hadn't stayed at their houses. Maybe the music business was different. Maybe it was just Travis.

"Sit and look at this," he said, already moved on from the topic of the apartment. "I want to know what you think."

I brought my drink to the island and sat down across from him, and for a second I was distracted again by how gorgeous he was and that a minute ago he'd been kissing me. *Really* kissing me, and his body had been against mine, and I had felt—

"The kiss was a good idea," he said, as if reading my mind. "I see what you're getting at if we want to sell this. We can't look like middle school kids at the school dance when we're out in public. We have to look like we're doing it."

"Uh, right." I couldn't help it when my gaze darted up toward the bedroom upstairs. Business. He was talking business.

"Like *really* doing it," Travis said. "You've got this good girl reputation, right? And you want to get rid of it. You want it to look like you dropped your panties for me. Like you're having this wild fling, and everyone thinks you've gone crazy, but the sex is so good that you've stopped caring what anyone thinks."

I nodded, mute. I didn't know what was wrong with me, because that suddenly sounded like a really good idea. The near-death experience had rewired my brain.

"I googled you, but I didn't see that you've done anything like that before," Travis continued as I stared at him in lust-filled silence. "There was something about a boyfriend, but that's it."

I cringed. "That was a few years ago. He's a producer. We dated for a while." It had actually been a year, and we broke up because he wanted me to quit acting and have his babies instead of a successful career. Far from feeling heartbroken, I was only annoyed that he had sucked up an entire year of my life.

"You've never hooked up with a co-star?" Travis asked.

"What? *No.*" I thought of Charlie Mackle, his tongue in my mouth, and recoiled in horror. Even Jimson Greer and his six-pack did nothing for me. "They're coworkers, not friends or boyfriends. It would be unprofessional. Acting is my job, not a dating app."

A smile touched the corner of Travis's perfect mouth. "I can see why you need a little rock n' roll to juice up your image. But I can work with this. We'll get you sexier roles."

"I don't want sexier roles. I want *the* role. The Holy Grail of roles. In Edgar Pinsent's next film."

Travis's eyebrows went up. "Really? I saw his last one, the World War Two one. It was intense."

"I've auditioned three times," I said. "I'm close, so close. But his assistant told my agent that Edgar says I'm too sweet to cast."

"Fuck him," Travis said. "Didn't he see *Party of Two*, where you're trying to seduce the guy with the bad haircut? You cut the hem off your dress to make it shorter, and you tugged the shoulder down to show your bra strap, and you did this sexy walk in heels. It was straight-up fucking hot."

My brain went blank. "You watched one of my movies?"

"I watched all of your movies," Travis said. "I think I liked *Sweet Summer Vacation* best, because the speedboat scene was so funny. Your comedy skills are killer. But then there's the scene where you're helping your mom after your dad died, and you made it bittersweet, happy and sad at the same time. I teared up, and it wasn't just because of the weed gummy."

I wasn't computing much of what he was saying. My brain was stuttering.

I was a successful actress. I had steady work. I had fans. I even had KatieWatch.

But I had never dated a man who had watched any of my movies.

Not ever.

Not even the producer I'd dated for a year.

Because even when a man liked me enough to date me, it was beneath him to sit all the way through one of my *silly romcom* movies. Every time.

And this man—Travis White, the freaking rock star—had watched all of them. It was suddenly very difficult not to crawl over this kitchen island and tackle him to the floor.

He hadn't noticed that he had just blown my mind. He was still talking business.

"Okay, so we get Edgar Pinsent to cast you," he was saying.

"What's the role?"

I cleared my throat. "I don't know. No one has read the script yet. I only know that whatever the role is, I want it."

Travis didn't question this. He nodded. "I wrecked the script you wrote for us, and I feel bad about that. You worked hard on it."

We should do more kissing, was all I could think. *Starting as soon as possible.* "Um, that's okay. The script had some problems. I realize that now." Breakfast? Had I actually thought that going for breakfast with Travis would change my image?

"I came up with other things, as an apology," Travis said. He pointed to the page in his notebook. "I listed ideas."

I tore my gaze from his face and squinted at the page. Travis's handwriting looked like someone had attempted to murder him while he wrote the list. "I can't read that."

Travis pointed to one of the indecipherable blobs. "This says that you get a tattoo," he suggested.

I shook my head, but my gaze wandered to the edge of the snake tattoo coming out of his sleeve. So sexy. "No tattoos," I said.

He waggled his brows. "You would look hot with ink." But when I shook my head again, he moved on and pointed to another blob. "Fine. We'll see some local bands. That one's not negotiable. Portland has a rocking music scene."

"I'll do it." Being seen at a concert with my hot rock star boyfriend was perfect. I didn't know why I hadn't thought of it. Also, it sounded fun. "What else?"

"We hang around town like normal people." He leaned back in his chair, gesturing expansively. "The way I see it, you've left L.A. for a getaway. A vacation. You left the pressure and the bullshit behind, and you're hanging out here, enjoying life while I fuck you every night. And every morning, too. Change up your wardrobe a bit—not a lot, but a little. Looser stuff, layers, not much makeup, your hair natural like you just rolled out of bed with me. And every time we're out, I'm all over you. Like I'm obsessed, right? Everyone will think that not only are you having this fling, you're completely rocking my world. People will love it."

I was nearly speechless again. "I'm rocking your world?"

"Oh yeah." Travis warmed to the topic, his blue eyes lit up with mischief. "Katie, you're not only owning it, you're a sex goddess. Confident. You take no shit. You get what you want, when you want it, and you don't apologize for it. I'm addicted. I'm completely whipped, and I'm loving it, and I don't care who knows. If we can pull it off, it'll be hot. You won't be romcom girl anymore."

I swigged my smoothie, because I was suddenly so turned on it was embarrassing. I had come up with dinner at Nobu, and Travis had come back with *sex goddess*. Me, a sex goddess.

I could do it. I could be that woman—the one who brought Travis White to his knees and made him drool for her. I could play her. I *wanted* to play her. Part of me also wanted to be her, for real.

"Well?" Travis asked, because I had been silent too long. "What do you think?"

I put my empty drink down and said the thought that crowded my mind, no matter how I tried to distract myself from it. "There's only one bed in this apartment."

He waved that away. "Oh, right. I'll sleep on the sofa, don't worry. It's just pretend."

I nodded. That made sense. When I impulsively came to Portland, it wasn't because I wanted to share a bed with Travis. I wasn't actually having an ill-advised fling with him. It was just pretend.

My gaze darted to the sofa. It looked large and comfortable. "I'm your guest, though. I could—"

"No, Katie." He shook his head. "Not happening. I've slept in worse places than that sofa. I'll be fine."

Were we really doing this? It looked like we were.

"Show me your notes," I said, motioning for his messy notebook. "And tell me your ideas. I'm listening."

TEN

Travis

AFTER A DECADE AS A ROCK STAR, I knew when a woman was coming on to me.

Katie Armstrong was *not* coming on to me.

There was a moment—when she grabbed me and kissed me—that I thought it was happening. I'd had every straight, single man's reaction when a beautiful woman pulls him in for a kiss: *Yes! This is happening! Let's go for it! I can't believe my luck!*

Then reality set in, and I knew why she was doing it. Because we had an agreement, because she thought I was hot, because we were fake dating. Also because, for a few minutes, she had thought she was going to die.

I had still kissed her back, of course. You only live once, and if Katie Armstrong was going to kiss me, then I would make it worth her while, even if it wasn't because she liked me. I'd been kissed for worse reasons than hers.

Still, there had been a moment—a fraction of a second—

when I had believed it. And it had felt good. It had felt weirdly like joy.

Katie had ditched her script, ditched L.A., and flown to Portland—and now I understood. A role with Edgar Pinsent was a big deal. She wasn't here for me. Aside from my obvious hotness, why would she be? I was a means to an end. I had, in fact, agreed to be a means to an end, and to use her the same way. I didn't need to screw this up by trying to fuck her—something she'd already said no to.

"I'm going to follow you on Instagram," Katie said, taking out her phone.

"Okay." I pulled groceries out of the fridge and set them on the counter to make us sandwiches. Katie still sat at the kitchen island.

She glanced up at me. "You don't understand, Travis. Get your phone. You have to follow me back, and you have to do it the minute after I follow you."

I lifted my hand from the lettuce. "What?"

"It's basically an announcement that we're dating," she explained. "We follow each other. But if I follow first, and you don't follow back immediately, it looks like you don't care about me as much as I care about you. People will think you treat me like dirt. They'll say we're doomed."

I stared at her. "You get all of that from an Instagram follow? Who even pays attention to who's following who?"

"*People.*" Her tone was exasperated. "Travis, *people* pay attention. You have over three million followers, and you only follow six people. Everyone will notice when you follow me." She tapped her phone. "Wait. One of the people you follow is... Sabrina Lowe."

"Probably. I don't remember." I picked up the loaf of bread, and then I saw Katie's stricken expression. I remembered how she'd made me promise I wasn't seeing anyone. "Babe, Sabrina and I didn't date long, and she's been my ex for months. She tossed me like week-old deli meat, and she had good reasons. I was being a dick to everyone I knew, especially her. She decided not to put up with my shit anymore. That doesn't mean I hate her."

Katie nodded, then shook her head, as if arguing with herself in her head. "Okay, but you have to unfollow her."

"Why?"

"Because she's Sabrina Lowe. She's one of the most beautiful pop stars in the world, and people will think you're not over her."

"How the hell will they get that from the fact that I follow her on Instagram?"

"They will, trust me."

"This is weird," I complained, but I put the bread knife down and retrieved my phone from the living room. "I don't get this social media stuff."

"But I do," Katie shot back. "So follow my lead."

I opened Instagram. The post I'd made from the road had thousands of likes and comments. I skipped those and found my following list. I unfollowed Sabrina, looked up Katie, and followed her. "There," I said. "Now *you* can take too long to follow *me*."

Katie gasped and rushed to follow me back.

A wave of notifications popped up, based on the fact that apparently no one had a life. I closed the app and put my phone down. I braced my arms on the counter and looked at Katie. "It looks like we just started dating," I said.

Our gazes locked. Katie's cheeks were flushed pink, her eyes bright. She looked beautiful. I should probably stop staring.

"I guess so," she said. "Now what? Are we going out tonight?"

I shook my head. "You just got here." I picked up the bread knife and pointed to my phone with it. "We did the Instagram thing after round one, but we're not going only one round. If you came all the way here for me, then I'd fuck you until late, until we're both exhausted." I paused, because that sounded hot and really good. "In the script," I clarified. "That's how it happens in the script. In real life, I'm making you a sandwich."

Katie's cheeks had gone deeper red, her lips parted. "Right. What happens tomorrow?"

"Tomorrow, we improvise," I told her. "That's part of this, Good Girl. No plans. We roll out of bed late—after I fuck you again, of course—and then we decide what we want to do. Like rock stars."

She put her elbows on the island and put her forehead into her hands. "I'm not good at being unscheduled."

"I am." I sliced the bread and moved on to a tomato. "I've been unscheduled for a while now. You're good at social media, but I'm good at being a guy with nothing to do but have fun. You'll see."

On the counter, both of our phones started buzzing and vibrating. Katie's phone nearly jumped over the edge. She picked it up. "Stella," she said to me. "I've been avoiding her."

I picked up my phone and read who was calling. "Jonathan," I said.

We exchanged a grin.

"You go first," I told her.

Katie tapped the phone and put it on speaker. "Hi, Stella."

"There you are!" Stella barked. "I just saw your Instagram. What the fuck is going on? I thought Travis White bailed on us."

"Surprise," I said, laying out bread slices.

"He's there?" Stella's voice moved away. "Jonathan, hang up. Katie's with Travis. They're on the phone."

My phone stopped vibrating, and Jonathan's voice came over the speaker. "Travis? I thought you left town."

"I did," I said. "I'm in Portland. With Katie."

"What?" Stella's voice went dangerously high.

"Jesus, Stella," Jonathan said. "Can't you keep tabs on your client?"

"Shut up," Stella shot back. "You didn't even know what city yours is in."

"Why are you two together?" Katie asked. She put her chin into her hands and watched me put sandwiches together. I held up the sliced turkey and raised my eyebrows. *Vegetarian?* I mouthed the word. She shook her head.

"We're in my office," Stella said. "Jonathan showed up when he couldn't get in touch with *his client.* He thought Travis might be with Katie. We were just discussing it—"

"Arguing about it," Jonathan put in.

"Whatever. Then the Instagram thing happened. So we called."

"Does everyone just stare at Instagram?" I asked, taking out the mayo, holding it up, and putting it back when Katie shook her head. "Katie says everyone does."

"It's my job," Stella snapped. "Katie, why are you in Portland with Travis? Is the deal back on? Is that why you're following each other?"

Katie and I exchanged a look. We hadn't discussed whether we'd tell our agents the truth. It was kind of tempting to let Stella and Jon believe they were interrupting us in bed. I shrugged at Katie, letting her know it was her call.

She took a breath. "Travis invited me to stay with him," she said. "I decided to take him up on it. I wanted to get out of L.A. for a while."

"You did?" Stella asked. "We didn't discuss it."

"It was a spur-of-the-moment decision," Katie said. "I'm taking a break."

"With Travis," Stella said.

"With Travis," Katie replied, and our gazes locked again. I waggled my eyebrows. She suppressed a smile.

"Travis," Jonathan broke in, "what are you doing in Portland? I didn't know you'd ever been there."

"I've played plenty of shows here," I said, stacking our sandwiches and lifting the bread knife to cut them. "I came here to work on a solo album."

There was silence from all three of the other people on the call. Katie's lips parted in surprise.

"There's an album in the works?" Jonathan sounded delighted, probably because for the first time in our association, I might actually make him some money.

"Well, I just got here," I said. "But I've talked to Finn Wiley. He's going to set me up at the Road Kings' studio."

"You *hate* the Road Kings," Jon said.

I nodded. "I do. That reminds me—I'm going to need a guitar. Mine are in storage back in L.A."

"I'll get one of your guitars out of storage," Jon said immediately. "Just tell me where to go and which one you want." The promise of a paycheck made him suddenly friendly.

I handed Katie her sandwich on a plate and made a thoughtful humming sound. "Actually, I don't want one of those. I'll buy a new guitar. There are lots of great music stores here."

"Do you have funds for a new guitar?" Jon said. "I'll make sure you have funds. Give me a couple of days, tops. Where are you staying? Do you have enough to get by?"

Katie was watching me, ignoring her sandwich. Her lips were still parted. She looked somewhat in awe.

"I'm covered for a place to stay," I said. "I might need a few other things, though. I'm going to be here a while."

"Whatever you need. You'll have it," Jon said.

"Excuse me," Stella broke in, annoyed. "Katie, what about your work schedule? When are you coming back to L.A.? I have people waiting for answers."

Katie looked at me. Then she sat straighter, putting her shoulders back. "I'm taking a break," she told Stella, her voice polite but firm. "I'll be back for *The Love Fix-Up* promo work, but that's it."

"What about these scripts?" Stella asked.

"No," Katie said. "No to the mom script. No to the plumber script. No to the cheer coach and to the Montana thing. No to all of them. If something good comes to you, then send it, and I'll decide. But in the meantime, I'm taking time to rethink the direction of my career."

To her credit, Stella only hesitated for a second, swallowing that news. But she couldn't quite help herself. "How much time? I need specifics."

"I don't have specifics," Katie said, and she only winced a little bit as she said it. "I just...need some time off for once. And you can forget about the replacements for Travis."

There were replacements for me? She had been thinking about a different fake boyfriend? The hell with that.

"All right," Stella said. "Call me later, Katie. We'll talk. If you need anything else, I'm here."

After we hung up, Katie sat in silence, as if surprised. "I can't believe I just did that," she said softly. "I haven't taken a break in over ten years. And she just... said yes."

"Welcome to the rock star life, Katie," I said. "You were born for it."

She smiled. Then she picked up her sandwich and dug in.

ELEVEN

Katie

WHEN I WOKE on my first official morning as Travis White's fake girlfriend, the apartment was quiet. I was alone in bed, of course, because my fake boyfriend wasn't in here with me. He had slept on the sofa, as he'd promised.

He hadn't looked put out when we went to bed last night. He'd just dug a spare sheet, pillow, and blanket out of a closet, made up the sofa, and said, "Night, Katie," as if we'd been roommates for years. I'd climbed the stairs to the loft bedroom feeling vaguely disappointed, even though if he'd tried something, I would have said no. Probably.

My brain had no logic when it came to him. I'd been clear that I wasn't going to sleep with him, and then I'd lain in bed in my pajamas, staring at the ceiling and thinking about the hot rock star downstairs, likely sleeping in—what, exactly? I was dying to know what he slept in, if anything. *Sex with Travis*

White? Jeez, no thanks. I'm too stupid for that! What do you think I am, anyway? A single, straight woman with eyes? It isn't like he's a good kisser or anything.

Either I was being smart or I was the dumbest woman alive. I fell asleep undecided.

I could smell coffee downstairs, but I didn't hear any sounds. When I looked at my phone on the nightstand, it was almost ten. I couldn't remember the last time I had slept this late—I was usually working back-to-back shoots.

I walked to the top of the stairs, glancing down at my pajama shorts and matching pajama T-shirt. Both were loose-fitting, so Travis wouldn't get too much of a show. I tried not to overthink it, and then I started down the stairs. Halfway down, I stopped.

In the loft, I could see the entire downstairs from above. There was coffee on in the kitchen. A steaming cup sat on the coffee table in the living room. And there, on the sofa, sprawled half out of the blanket, was Travis White, bathed in the golden morning light streaming in the windows.

Travis was awake, but his limbs were lazily stretched out. One bare leg had escaped the blanket, and I could see all the way to the hem of his boxer briefs. He had on a T-shirt, but one arm was bent behind his head, showing the full ink of his tattoos, all the way up his biceps. He was leaning back against the cushions, intent, his blue eyes fixed on the book he held in his other hand. As I watched, he turned the page.

The sexiest man I had ever seen was…reading. Every single part of me woke up. Even my toes were turned on.

I descended a few more steps, and Travis looked up from his book. "Morning," he said in that smoky, deep voice. His gaze moved up and down me in an unmistakable way, and then fixed on my face. "Coffee's on in the kitchen."

"Ah hah," I said stupidly, then cleared my throat. "I mean, sounds good."

He didn't move any part of his body except his eyes as he watched me walk to the kitchen. I self-consciously searched the unfamiliar cupboards for a mug. "Good book?" I asked to break the silence.

"Maybe," Travis replied.

"You don't know?" I poured my coffee and walked to the living room. There was nowhere to sit except for the sofa. Travis slid his feet back, bending his knees and giving me room. The rest of him stayed sprawled where it was.

I sat. The blanket was warm from his body heat—or maybe that was just my lust-filled body. We were sitting on the sofa in our sleepwear, our bodies only inches apart.

I almost sipped my coffee, decided it was too hot, and put it down on the table. I had no desire to sputter hot coffee in front of him. "So. Wild night, huh?"

Those remarkably blue eyes blinked once, and then Travis grinned. He knew how crazy the situation was, innocent and hot at the same time. "Wild," he agreed. "The best I ever had, baby."

"I mean, *wow*," I said. "I'm sore all over."

"You better be," he said.

I picked up my coffee and swigged it, heat be damned.

Travis didn't say anything else. He just watched me drink and put the cup down again. I couldn't tell what he was thinking.

My gaze dropped to the book he was reading. "*A Tale of Two Cities?*" I asked him. He was reading Dickens? A classic? My ovaries couldn't take any more of this onslaught. They cried for mercy.

"Yeah." He shrugged. "That's why I don't know if it's good. It's hard to understand. But I'm trying."

"I haven't read it since high school. I don't remember it very well."

"I only passed high school because I cheated," Travis said. "So now I read books. It's an attempt to improve my intellect. I have no idea if it's working."

I tried to hide my shock. "You *cheated?*"

The grin touched the corner of his perfect mouth. "You didn't?"

"I never even skipped a class."

Something flared in Travis's eyes. "Oh, baby," he said, his voice low and smoky. "Talk dirty to me."

"Stop it," I said, laughing and turned on at the same time. "Or I'll tell the world that you're secretly a nerd. How do rock stars have time to read classics, anyway?"

"Lots of hours on planes, in airports, in hotels, and backstage," he replied. "The high points are high, but a lot of it is boring."

I nodded. "So it's like being on set between takes."

"Probably. What do you read on set between takes, Katie?"

Did he really want to know? Yes, he did. It was a question no other boyfriend had asked me, just like no other boyfriend had watched my movies. "I'd like to read more novels, but usually I read scripts," I answered him. "I'm always lining up the next job."

"You need work that bad?" he asked. "You seem successful to me."

"I am, but it could end any minute," I said. "Nothing is guaranteed. The industry could change. The market could change. I'm in my thirties, and women have an expiry date. If I'm being offered work, I have to take it before it all goes away. That's the acting business."

Travis rested the book on his chest and looked thoughtful. Before he could speak, I plunged on.

"The music business is the same in some ways, I guess," I said. "But you're a man. You can make music and get laid into your seventies."

"The fuck," he protested softly. "That sounds horrible. I'm way too lazy to work that long."

"Maybe, but you have the option. I don't. So I work."

He was watching me, his gaze calm, and I felt like he could see straight into my head. "So it's like you said yesterday," he said. "You've never taken a break before."

I shook my head. "I've never been able to afford it."

"And can you afford it now?"

"Financially, yes," I replied. "But this break is a gamble, Travis. I *need* Edgar Pinsent. He liked my auditions. Now he's refinancing the project and rewriting the script, so I have another chance. If I land Edgar Pinsent—if I work with one of Hollywood's most prestigious directors on a movie that will win Oscars—then I don't have to worry all the time. My career will be made."

Travis scratched his jaw, thinking. His hand moved slowly. I watched. Even his fingers were beautiful, long and graceful, the nails clean and trim.

"Got it," he said. "Get dressed, babe. Let's get this done."

WE STARTED by going for coffee at the hipster coffee shop downstairs. When Travis saw what I was wearing—jeans and a button-down shirt with a belt—he not only sent me back to change, he came up to the loft's bedroom and went through my suitcase himself.

He made no comment on my underwear or my pack of birth control pills. I breathed silently through the embarrassment, reminding myself that if this was my actual boyfriend, nothing in my suitcase would shock him. Finally, Travis pulled out a cotton camisole and held it up. "Wear this," he said.

"That's underwear," I argued.

He frowned in confusion. "It's a top."

"It's an indoor top," I insisted. "It's called lounge wear."

"You can't lounge outside?" His eyebrows went up. "Seems to me that you can. Keep the jeans, but change your shirt. We'll add another layer."

I snatched the camisole from his hand. "Fine, but turn your back. You're not getting a free show."

He turned his back, and I unbuttoned my shirt, slid it off, and put the camisole on. "This is too revealing," I complained. "I'm not going to dress slutty all of a sudden. Also, it's March."

"You have no faith in my vision," Travis said, turning around. His gaze zeroed in on my breasts for a second, even though I wore a bra under the camisole. Then he wrenched his eyes up to my face. "I am the Edgar Pinsent of sluttiness, Katie," he proclaimed. "I'm an artist."

That was charming, I had to admit. "But sluttiness isn't my style," I still protested as he turned to my suitcase again.

"Silence," he ordered as he looked through my clothes. He held out a cream-colored cardigan, made of soft cashmere, one of my favorite things in my wardrobe. "Put this on." He found a necklace. "And this."

Once I had all of it on, I had to admit that I liked what I saw in the bedroom's full-length mirror. The camisole was sexy where it peeked from the sweater, enough to be evocative but not over the top. It emphasized my throat and just enough cleavage while not revealing too much. My only makeup was mascara and lip gloss.

Travis stood behind me as I looked in the mirror. He wore jeans, a tee, and a plaid shirt unbuttoned over it, the cuffs rolled up his forearms, and he effortlessly looked like the sexiest man who had ever lived. He hadn't shaved this morning to perfect the sex-marathon look. I wanted to lick him, but he didn't notice. "Your hair," he said.

"There's nothing wrong with my hair."

He shook his head and tutted. "Babe, you've never had sex hair? Come on."

"Sex hair?" I said, worried, but he was already touching my hair where I'd put it neatly up, loosening strands. He placed a few wisps across my forehead and arranged more at the back of my neck.

When he had finished, I nearly gasped at the sight of myself. The effect was subtle, but it was *hot*. I was hot.

Was this what I was supposed to look like after sleeping with a man? I had never looked like this, even after falling into bed with someone. For me, sex—even good sex—had always been followed by proper sleep hygiene and a tidy look the next day. Then again, even good sex had always been over by eleven p.m. This look said that we'd gone until at least three, then woken up at seven to go again.

Was this what all of Travis's girlfriends had looked like? His real ones?

I wasn't going to think about that.

Before leaving, I put on my trench and Travis slid on a beat-up leather jacket. He added Ray-Bans, the pricey sunglasses contrasting with his low-cost outfit. He looked exactly like what he was—a rock star between gigs, getting coffee late on a weekday morning after (fictionally) having sex all night. He was irresistible.

People noticed. Heads turned in the coffee shop to follow us to the counter. Most of them stared at Travis, but a few of them stared at me. I put my own sunglasses on as we walked out into the sunny spring morning, cups in hand.

We started walking, our route aimless as we drank. It felt

awkward only for half a minute, and then it...wasn't. We started talking.

Travis was easy to talk to. He was interesting, funny, and smarter than he let on. He asked me questions, and when I when I talked his ear off in reply, he listened. An hour passed as if it were a few minutes as we took in the early-spring sunshine, the brisk air, and the bracing chill of Portland in March. Travis was stopped twice by fans asking for selfies, but other than a lot of looks, no one else bothered us, and I quickly forgot that we were supposed to be putting on a show.

When our coffees were empty and we had tossed the cups into a nearby trashcan, Travis took my hand in his. I stuttered as I felt his fingers gently clasp me. "Keep talking," he prompted when I was quiet too long.

We were holding hands in public. It was strange and awkward only for a moment, and then it was nice. I curled my fingers around him and felt myself relax. I didn't care about whether anyone noticed us. I was simply enjoying this.

It turned out that Travis White and I agreed on some very serious issues. One: Why anyone would scuba dive was beyond us, because the ocean was mostly unexplored and full of monsters, and humans didn't belong in it. Two: Caramel didn't need sea salt; it was good on its own. Three: Neither of us had ever eaten a piece of fruit from a fruit basket and would not do so even under duress, because you don't know who has touched that thing. Four: *Almost Famous* was the greatest movie of all time.

The important things.

As we walked the final block back to the apartment, Travis switched it up. He let go of my hand and slung his arm over my shoulders, tugging me gently against him. By instinct, and to keep my balance, my arm slid around his waist. It should have been stiff, with us bumping against each other, but it wasn't. We were in sync, and I knew we looked convincing. We looked like two lovers out for a post-coital stroll.

This was going to work.

I ignored the fact that he smelled good, that his body fit like a puzzle piece into mine. He was only a few inches taller than me, and his lean arm rested easily on my shoulders, his hand dangling. This was a man who didn't need to grip or grab a woman to claim her; he knew exactly what he was doing with minimal body language. I might be the actor of the two of us, but Travis White had been using his body onstage for years, in front of crowds of thousands, and he was fully in command of every part of it.

I had kissed and put my hands on a lot of very attractive men, but this was different. Travis's body under my arm was lithe and firm, and up close I could feel the inimitable way his hips moved. My skin prickled and I could suddenly feel my nipples under my clothes.

As I tried not to obsess over his sexy walk, Travis said casually, "We'll make some ground rules up front. No kissing in public unless we discuss it first."

I couldn't speak.

"We don't need to overdo it," Travis continued, oblivious. "We can look hot without crossing lines. Trust me. I'll sell it, but don't worry that I'm going to grab your ass."

It took a second for me to answer, because I was suddenly picturing his hand curving over me, taking its slow time, those fingers curling and squeezing. "Good to know," I said.

"However," Travis continued, "Feel free to grab mine anytime you like."

I sputtered a laugh. "Travis!"

"I'm just saying. I consent."

"I'm not going to grab your ass."

"Even if you're a woman breaking the rules on a wild fling?" he asked.

My face was burning. "Even then."

"Sure," he said skeptically. "We'll see."

TWELVE

Travis

I AWOKE to the sound of familiar bare feet descending the loft stairs. Even though the light in the windows was cloudy with drizzle, I knew I had slept late, because apparently I wasn't as young as I used to be.

"Travis." Katie's hiss-whisper was loud enough to be heard by the neighbors. "Are you awake? It's working."

I rolled over on the sofa—this fucking sofa, that I had slept on alone while Katie slept upstairs every night for the past week. It was a comfortable sofa, but the fact that it didn't include a naked Katie Armstrong was incurring more and more of my resentment. "What?" I asked as my brain stuttered to life.

Katie dropped onto the sofa near my feet. She was wearing her pajamas, and her hair was sleep-tousled. She'd been self-conscious on her first morning, but that was gone now. She leaned over me as I drew my feet back, holding her phone out for me to see, her eyes sparkling. Her shoulder pressed the inside of my bent knee, and her top dipped dangerously at this angle, giving me a glimpse of creamy skin.

I scrubbed a hand through my hair while making sure the blanket covered my lap. "Woman, why are you awake? I thought I wore you out last night."

Her cheeks flushed red. We'd gone to a club last night to check out an indie band. It was loud, the music was good, and we'd had a few drinks each. We hadn't gotten home until after one. I'd planned to wake up slowly today and stay as lazy as possible.

Katie decided to ignore my flirting and waved the phone in my face. "Look," she said.

I took her phone. TikTok was open, and there was a cell phone shot of Katie and me leaving the club last night, our hands clasped tight as we brushed through the crowd to the curb. I helped her into the Uber and closed the door.

It wasn't an overly interesting clip, though we both looked good. Katie had worn her hair down around her shoulders, and by the end of the night, it was curled and damp with sweat. It was sexy.

I glanced at the stats and did a double take. The clip had eight thousand likes and counting, not even twelve hours after the clip was posted. There were over seven hundred comments. The account that had posted it was called KatieWatch.

"What's this?" I asked aloud. I tapped into the KatieWatch page. "You have a TikTok account with twenty thousand followers?"

"It isn't mine," Katie explained. "It's a fan account. A week ago, it was a fraction that big. It started growing after the basketball game, and it's been going crazy since we followed each other on Instagram."

Social media was wild. I scrolled through the other videos on the page and saw the things Katie and I had been doing for the past week. We'd gotten dinner out a few times, we'd gone to a music store to buy me a guitar, and we'd gone shopping for an afternoon. It was all there.

"Is this person following us around?" I asked, concerned.

Katie punched my shoulder. "No. People send her their videos and she posts them. Look at the comments."

I tapped back into the video from last night and scanned the comments.

OMG, I am living for these two.

I don't know what's going on, but I am HERE FOR IT.

Have they made a statement yet? I want to know what's happening!

Katie is winning. Look at him!!

Our girl is getting it from the hottest man alive, and I couldn't be happier for her.

Is that Travis White? Holy hell.

I've never seen Katie look this hot! She's always gorgeous, but now she's smoking!

Where has Travis been? Looks like he's cleaned up his act. I'll bet Katie is a good influence on him.

He's got so many problems. I hope she doesn't get her heart broken.

I frowned at that last one, then handed the phone back, unable to read any more comments. "You're right," I said. "It looks like it's working."

"It is." She was vibrating with excitement, oblivious to the press of her shoulder against my knee. My knee was not oblivious, and neither was the rest of my body.

Over the past week, my mummified body had most definitely emerged from oblivion. Apparently, the one thing that could wake me up from the neck down was this beautiful woman who didn't want me except as a prop—a woman who had climbed me like a tree, then hadn't made a move since. My confused synapses veered from flirting to lustful pining to despair, sometimes in the course of a minute. Like now.

I wanted to make a move, but there was too much at risk. If Katie turned me down, we'd look tense together, and we didn't need that right when the plan was starting to work.

While I tortured myself over all of this, I ran out of time. Katie had to go back to L.A. today for promo shoots for *The Love Fix-Up*, as well as other obligations she had in her busy career. We hadn't planned out when we'd see each other again, because it was *my* stupid idea to play it loose and improvise this thing. I was kicking myself. I really did have a talent for screwing myself over.

"I think this is the perfect time for me to go back to L.A.," Katie said, putting her phone away. "We want it to look like I had a fling, but not like I've given up my whole life for a guy. Don't you think?"

"Right," I said, wishing I could push up that pajama top, press her back into the blankets, and fuck her until she couldn't breathe.

"Besides, I need to meet with Stella," Katie said. "To strategize. Travis, this has been amazing. I couldn't have hoped for a better fake boyfriend. You've been perfect."

Panic clutched in my chest. "Wait. Are we breaking up already?"

"Of course not." She smiled, leaning back, no longer pressing against me. It made me happy and sad at the same time. "It's just more believable if I go back to L.A. I think we should do an official PR announcement soon, and we should each do Instagram posts. Let me think about how to do it right."

"Okay," I said weakly.

"What time is it?" She was gearing into full professional mode now. "I'll shower, get dressed, and call a car for the airport."

"No," I countered, not ready to let her go just yet. "I'm driving you."

She shook her head. "You don't have to."

"I do," I argued. "My soon-to-be-Instagram-official girlfriend just spent a week with me. You think I'd kick her out to go to the airport alone? What am I, a monster? I'll drive you myself. I'll see you off."

Katie nodded. "Okay."

"And I'll kiss you," I added impulsively. "Be ready."

She went red again. "You said we'd discuss it first."

"We're discussing it now. Do you have an objection?"

She finally looked uneasy, as if she'd just noticed she was effectively in my bed with me. "Well—no. I don't object. I think —I think it works well with the script. You're right. If we've just spent a week together, it's romantic for you to see me off and kiss me goodbye."

"I'm glad you see it that way," I said. "It'll be a good one, I promise. Tongue or no tongue? I take requests."

"*Travis.*" She hesitated. "No tongue. This kiss is supposed to be romantic and sweet, not foreplay."

"Got it. Though for the record, I don't think it's fair that the pasty guy in *The Christmas Date* got foreplay, and so did the cowboy in *Bakin' Love*, but I don't."

Katie made a face. "Do you want the truth?"

"Always."

"The Christmas guy tasted like mustard, and the cowboy was gay."

I slapped my thigh. "I knew there was something off in that one. I should have guessed."

"He was a decent kisser." She shrugged. "But his boyfriend hanging out on set made it weird for the romantic scenes."

She had kissed a lot of men. I would have to up my game.

I was motivated, though. I thought that counted for something.

THIRTEEN

Katie

TRAVIS'S CAR WAS SEXY. There was no other word for it. It was vintage, painted dusky blue with two wide, white stripes on the hood. I knew nothing about cars, but even I knew that when he turned the key and the whole thing vibrated smoothly like it was about to fly to the moon, I loved this one.

Travis watched my face for a long moment as the engine purred. "Did you just have an orgasm?" he finally asked.

I felt my cheeks heat. "This car has more charisma than any boyfriend I've ever had," I admitted.

He laughed. "Until now. It's okay—I love it, too. It's a '69 Camaro, in case that means anything to you. Mint condition. It's the only thing I owned in my old life that I loved too much to sell."

I blinked at that. I saw Travis as carefree and impulsive, not actually broke. "You sold everything?" I asked.

He listed off, counting on his fingers. "The house in

Malibu. The other cars I bought—most of which I never drove. The New York apartment. The furniture was borrowed, and so was a lot of my wardrobe. It was a trip when the reps from the designers showed up to take all of their clothes back. They literally took my shoes."

I stared at him in shock, sitting there in this car in the parking garage under his borrowed apartment building. "Sorry if this is a rude question, but—how the hell did that happen?"

Travis shrugged and put the car into gear, pulling out of the parking spot. "The record company and the managers took most of the money I ever made. I had to pay lawyers—expensive lawyers. And with all the lawsuits, I couldn't afford to maintain the houses or the cars, anyway. It all had to go."

"Travis, that's terrible."

He pulled out into traffic. "It's life," he said. "My parents are hippies. Sometimes we had money growing up—when they held down jobs—and sometimes we didn't. When I was rich, they wouldn't take my money. Now that I'm broke again, they don't care about that, either. They're on a camping tour right now. The last I heard, they were in British Columbia, smoking weed somewhere in the mountains. It was a weird childhood, but at least it taught me not to care about material things." He paused. "Except for this car. I fucking *love* this car."

We had pulled into traffic, and I rolled my window down to let the fresh air in. I sensed that Travis didn't want to talk about his money problems in too much detail. "My parents won't take my money, either," I said. "I keep trying, but they refuse."

"Annoying, isn't it?" Travis said.

"So annoying. They live in Minnesota, in the same house I was born in. They've been married for forty years. My mom is a nurse, and my dad is a college professor. Neither of them plans to retire yet, even though I could help them do it. They say they like to keep busy."

"They sound like nice people," Travis said as we moved through traffic. We were only going to PDX, but it was still fun to take a ride in this car.

"They are nice." I paused, thinking about how to word it. "But they feel...distant somehow. Like they live on another planet. My brother lives a few blocks from my parents with his wife and their daughter. We're not as close as I wish we were."

"Hollywood is far away from everything in every possible way," Travis said. "It's like living on the International Space Station."

"Exactly." I stared at his profile, thinking how nice it was to be understood for once. "I mean, I like it. I love my job. It's the only thing I've ever wanted. But sometimes I go home to visit, and I think, *do I know this place?* I grew up there, but it feels like I don't belong. And even though I love my life, it makes me sad. Then I don't visit as much as I should, because of the sadness, and that just makes me sadder."

"Ah, the sadness that makes you sadder because you feel sad about being sad. I know it well."

My lips pressed into a smile. We stopped at a stoplight, and the guy in the car next to us did a double take. "Is the sadness why you were sitting naked by Andy Rockweller's pool?" I asked.

"Pretty much," Travis replied. "I thought I got clothes on before you saw me. I hope I didn't give you a show."

"You didn't." I could hear the regret in my voice. Travis laughed.

He was seeing me to the airport, where he was going to kiss me. We'd discussed it this morning on his sofa where he'd just woken up, the two of us pressed together. It had felt so comfortable that I hadn't felt self-conscious until I realized we were talking about kissing.

Despite how strange the setup was, everything about this week had been perfect. And now I was leaving.

Damn, there was the sadness again.

We were quiet for a while, an easy silence between us. We talked about inconsequential things, and then he was parking in the short-term parking lot. It was ending too fast. I hadn't had the chance to say—what? I didn't know what there was to say, only that I felt robbed of time, as if I wasn't going to see him again.

It was in the script that I'd see him again, because we hadn't broken up. But when?

I wasn't finished worrying about it when we got as far as Travis could go, close to the security line. He let go of the handle of my wheeled suitcase and turned to me.

I was still trying to come up with words, but Travis didn't need them. He lifted his hands, cupped my jaw gently, and kissed me.

I leaned up and kissed him back, drinking him in. His lips were warm and expert, familiar from the last time we'd kissed. His hands put the lightest pressure on my skin. I reached under his jacket and put my hands on his waist, rising up on my toes so I could kiss him better.

It lasted a long, sweet moment. Not long enough.

He pulled back, his mouth losing contact with mine. "No tongue," he said softly. "Just like we agreed."

Had he *wanted* to kiss me? People were staring, I was sure. Someone might have snapped a photo. But with his hands on my jaw and his body so close, I wasn't thinking about that. I was thinking only that I wanted to kiss him more, and I regretted that I'd had all week to do it. I should have kissed him every day, and now I was losing my chance.

For a second, as his blue eyes looked into mine, I was sure he felt the same way.

Travis hesitated, as if he was considering kissing me again. Then he stepped back and dropped his hands.

"See you later, Katie," he said.

"Bye," I answered, my voice a whisper, but the crowd swirled in and he was already gone.

WHEN I GOT BACK to my apartment in L.A., I immediately texted my part-time assistant, Gwen. *I need wardrobe help,* I wrote. *Can you come over?*

She responded immediately. *I need to TALK TO YOU!!!! I'll be there in twenty.*

I washed up and unzipped my suitcase as I waited for her. I didn't need a full-time assistant, but I often needed help, especially when I was in the middle of shooting and working long hours. When I needed it, Gwen made sure my fridge was full, my clothes were cleaned and pressed, and my hair and nail appointments were made. My parents had raised me to look after myself, and I was hard-wired not to be completely helpless. I didn't want to be one of those Hollywood people who can't make a doctor's appointment or renew a driver's license, someone who doesn't know how much groceries cost. I did most things myself, but with Gwen's help so it didn't become too much.

This worked for Gwen, who was twenty-four and—in her words—"didn't want to be tied down to only one gig." I certainly didn't pay her enough to live on her own in L.A., and I didn't know what else she did to make ends meet. I had the feeling the answer to that question changed from week to week. I only knew that Gwen was experienced, discreet, trustworthy, and for some reason, she hadn't quit.

She had stocked my fridge, because I'd given her my flight

information. She also had a key to my apartment, so as I spooned yogurt and granola into a bowl, she walked in without knocking. "Travis *White?*" she said.

Gwen was short and curvy, and somehow she made high-waisted jeans look like she was a 1950s movie starlet. She could also pull off a pixie cut like no one I'd ever seen. She looked me up and down from behind her thick-framed, stylish glasses, and I instantly felt judged.

I straightened my spine, remembering my role. *Sex goddess*, I reminded myself. "Travis White," I affirmed, digging my spoon into my bowl. "Thanks for stocking the fridge."

"You're welcome," Gwen said. "What's this about wardrobe help?"

"I think it's time to change it up."

Her eyebrows rose. "You mean you're finally ready to stop dressing like my high school math teacher?"

I lowered my bowl. "I don't dress that bad!"

She shrugged. "You dress a little geeky. You pull it off because you're hot." She waved up and down, indicating me. "But it needs work. I can help." She walked past me into my bedroom, sliding the closet door open.

I followed, eating my snack. I didn't know what I wanted, exactly, only that I had the itch to look different after the week I'd had.

Gwen had her back to me as she rifled through my closet like someone who had been in here plenty of times, putting away my dry cleaning. "You and Travis followed each other on Instagram," she said. "That's basically a wedding announcement."

"I like him," I said, which was true.

"I did you a favor," she said without looking back at me. "I asked around about him. I figured someone should, since apparently you decided to get on a plane just to sleep with him. You date so rarely, you don't know what you're doing."

"What do you mean, you asked around?"

That got me an amused glance over her shoulder. "Assistants know everything, Katie. My neighbor's roommate's sister works for Sabrina Lowe. He says that when Sabrina and Travis were together, they weren't hot and heavy. They saw each other maybe once a week, if that, and he never spent the night."

I shoved a spoonful of yogurt and granola into my mouth, not wanting to admit how relieved I was that Travis hadn't been *hot and heavy* with the most beautiful woman in pop music. That he might not be heartbroken over her.

"My roommate's GrubHub driver's sister is Andy Rockweller's cleaning lady," Gwen went on, pulling clothes on hangers from my closet and laying them on the bed. "She says that since Travis has been staying in Andy's house, he hasn't been partying and he hasn't had any women over. At all."

"That's personal information," I protested.

"You think we don't know what's going on?" Gwen said. "You think we don't know who's in bed with who, who's drunk, who's about to get a divorce? We know who's cheating, who's gay, and who's so awful that no one will work for them anymore. And we talk. Not to exchange gossip, but for survival. It's a whisper network."

That was a lot to process. I should probably worry about what Gwen told the whisper network about me, but my brain was stuck on the fact that Travis hadn't been lying when he told me he hadn't been sleeping around. I felt myself let go of worry I hadn't realized I'd been carrying. Travis was famous and he was freaking beautiful. He could have anyone. The fact that he hadn't—I didn't know why I cared, but I did.

Then I wondered why he'd been so alone. We had talked

about sadness on the way to the airport. How depressed had he been?

"What else did you learn about Travis?" I asked, leaving my morals behind and deciding I didn't actually want to know what Gwen said about me. Ever.

Gwen looked down at the clothes she'd spread on the bed, her hands on her hips. "No drugs at the moment, no weird sexual habits, no prescriptions, and no personality disorders," she replied.

"What? How do you know his psychiatric diagnosis?"

Gwen held up a hand. "Trust," was her only explanation. "The negatives are that he's definitely broke, or close to it, so he might be using you for money. Also, he went off the rails when his band broke up. Drinking and punching people and wrecking things. But my sources say that behavior has cleared up. He hasn't been drinking at Andy Rockweller's or using any drugs. Andy Rockweller has been sober for decades. Also, my sources know other sources who know who scores what in this town, and Travis's name isn't on any of those lists."

"You're terrifying me right now," I said. "Are Hollywood assistants part of the mafia?"

"No, we're just not oblivious. So give me the scoop, Katie. Is he good in bed, or what?"

My face went red-hot. "I'm not telling you that. Sabrina Lowe's second cousin's Uber driver will know before you leave this apartment."

Gwen looked me up and down again. "I can't decide. Considering you just spent a week in that snack's bed, you don't look orgasmed out."

"I *am*. I am orgasmed out. But I'm going back to work, so I need to be professional again."

"Okay." Gwen motioned to the clothes she'd laid out—tops,

dresses, sweaters, blazers, skirts. "What are we doing with your clothes?"

I stared at the clothes, and suddenly I didn't want to put any of them on ever again. I thought of how I had looked in Travis's mirror, with my camisole and sex hair. I felt an ache low in my belly at the thought of being *orgasmed out*, but I ignored it. My chance had passed.

"I want to look sexy, but in a way that's still me," I said, the words coming out raw and almost sad. "I don't feel the same as I did before. It isn't about dressing for him. It's about dressing for me. I want to look at myself and think I'm hot. Not smart and responsible and hardworking. *Hot.*"

Behind the lenses of her glasses, Gwen's gaze softened, and she lost some of her attitude. Then she nodded as if she understood. "Yeah, Katie," she said. "We can do that."

FOURTEEN

Travis

ON A TRIP to a music store during the week Katie was here, I had bought an acoustic guitar. It was beautiful. I hadn't played it for Katie—I'd kept it in its case and propped in a corner of the apartment, as if it was just another belonging. I hadn't wanted to admit to her that it was so long since I'd played that I was terrified I was out of practice. I wasn't even sure I remembered how to play at all.

Guitar had been my first love. My dad had bought me a guitar for my thirteenth birthday—a random gift that he'd bought secondhand for cheap. I'd bypassed taking lessons and taught myself, in the time-honored way of sitting alone with headphones, listening to my favorite songs and trying to make the guitar make the same sounds. I could have gotten someone to teach me, but why make it easy when it can be stupid and hard?

I'd discovered, when I sang along to the songs I played

badly, that my voice wasn't bad. With the reckless confidence of a fourteen-year-old, I had started a band.

Over the years of being immersed in music as a career, I'd learned other instruments and picked up some actual knowledge. But with a bass player and two guitarists in Seven Dog Down, I wasn't required to play guitar onstage, just sing. I played in my down time because I liked it, and I played some of the tracks in studio when we recorded our albums, but it was made clear to me that as the frontman, I was expected to show up and deliver, not play with any skill.

After the band broke up, I'd thought about getting one of my guitars and going back to the basics, figuring out why I loved music again. But I hadn't done it. I had stared at Andy's pool instead.

I'd talked big about making a solo album, but I was good at talking big. Now that Katie had gone back to L.A. and I was alone in this apartment, there was no more talk. There was no Andy, no pool to stare into. Just this nice studio, and the rainy Portland day outside, and my own thoughts in my head. In other words, a fucking nightmare.

I opened the case and stared at the guitar. It stared back. I thought of all the people waiting for me to do something—my fans, my three million Instagram followers, my agent, my crying bank account, all the people I owed money and favors to—and had a long, hard moment of panic. Sweat dampened my temples.

Put up or shut up, I told myself. *Time to do the fucking thing.*

I took a deep breath. I had the urge to get drunk. I hadn't thought about drugs in a long time, but suddenly I missed them so much it was like my dog had died. A Valium to take the edge off. An Adderall to make my thoughts sharp. When you first did coke, there was a moment, right before the crash, when you felt like you could do *anything*.

I scrubbed the heels of my hands over my eyes. "Fuck off," I said aloud, maybe to myself, maybe to the guitar, maybe to the fictional coke I didn't have. Then I dropped my hands and picked up the guitar.

At first, it felt right. Good, even. Like—I imagined—when you snug your own kid into your lap and feel them relax. My hands knew what to do, and I strummed a few chords, picked at the notes, then tuned the guitar, working from automatic memory. I did know how to do this.

I tried "Heaven's Gate," one of Seven Dog Down's big hits, a song I had performed a hundred times onstage. We'd never done a show without it. My hands flew. I knew this song like I knew my own heartbeat, even though I hadn't written it. I didn't even like it all that much, to be honest. But I knew it.

The notes came out, but my hands started to cramp. My fingertips hurt on the fret, and the hand holding the pick got slick with sweat. The notes slowed down, jarred out of rhythm.

I tried again, then again. I switched songs. I could hear it in my head, but my hands got worse and worse. Too late, I remembered that guitar playing trains your hands the same way that running trains your legs. I hadn't played in so long, and I was a runner who had been sitting on the sofa for a year, going for his first run, aching and out of breath.

Eventually—I had no idea how much time had passed—I put the guitar down. My hands were screaming, and my left fingers were starting to bleed. I got up, stopped the kitchen sink, and dumped a tray of ice into it. I ran cold water over the ice and dunked my hands in, feeling the cold slice through the pain. Thin tendrils of blood swirled over the ice.

I started to cry, because what the fuck? I was a mess. I was nothing like anyone believed I was. They all thought I was a musician, and I couldn't fucking play. What musician can't play his own guitar? I'd had to borrow the money to buy the guitar in the first place and then play it all alone in this borrowed apartment. I was a phony, a fake. I had never deserved fame, and I knew it better than anyone.

I stood there with tears running down my face until I couldn't feel my hands anymore. I lifted my hands out of the ice and grabbed two tea towels. Moving the guitar aside, I lay on the sofa. I turned on Netflix and wrapped each hand in a tea towel, lying there like an invalid, my self-pity deeper than the ocean.

I watched *The Christmas Date*, and when Katie came onscreen, I felt something twist deep behind my breastbone. She was so fucking beautiful. I had taken her to the airport, and I had kissed her, because that was our deal. She wanted someone who made her look edgy and sexy and cool. That was me, because I was all appearances and no substance. A musician who had no career and couldn't play. And I needed her, because in every aspect of my life, I was a failure.

Katie couldn't fix what was wrong with me. She didn't know how much I had liked kissing her, and even if she learned of it, she wouldn't care. Worse, she would be horrified. I was a means to an end for her, just like I'd been a means to an end for every manager, agent, lawyer, bandmate, girlfriend, and record company executive who had used me over the last decade. A good-looking piece of ass and not much else.

The Christmas Date made me feel a little better despite myself. I stopped crying, at least. That was the magic of Katie and her movies, why her fans loved her so much. A lot of them had probably done what I was doing now, turned on one of her movies in a low moment. There was a scene where Katie was hanging Christmas lights and realized—once she's at the top of a ladder—that she's afraid of heights. The way she gripped the ladder with her knees, then tried to slither down while plastered to the steps in terror, was a master class in physical comedy. My girl was fucking funny.

My fake girl.

My phone rang on the coffee table, and I could see from the display that it was Finn. I unwrapped one aching hand just enough to tap the answer button and put him on speaker, and then I wrapped my hand again. "Hey, man," I managed.

"Hey," Finn said. "I'm downstairs and I'm coming up. Are you naked?"

"Listen," I said. "I really don't like you that way. It's time to move on."

"Oh, you're hilarious. Why am I on speaker?"

"Because I'm in the middle of an orgy and my hands are full. Is this urgent? I'm about to empty the lube."

"Jesus, Travis. Thirty seconds." He hung up.

Finn had the code to the place, because it was his. When he came through the door and saw me in my prone position on the sofa, a Netflix romcom playing, he paused. "What happened to your hands?" he asked.

"I got blood on one of your tea towels. Sorry. I'll wash it out."

I heard him come into the living room, and then he was standing next to the sofa, looking down at me. "Ah. The guitar," he said, spotting it in its open case on the floor.

"Leave me alone, man." I was irrationally glad that I had stopped crying and my face had dried. At least I had that. "Today is a bad day. Come back later."

Finn ignored me and picked up my left hand, unwrapping it. "Ouch," he said. "Keep playing. The calluses will come back. Why are you watching a Christmas movie?"

"It's what I have instead of drugs," I replied. "Do you have any cocaine? I would like some."

"Travis." Finn put my hand back down. "What did we agree about coke when we were in Paris all those years ago?"

I sighed. "It's always a bad idea."

"The worst idea," Finn agreed. "If you score, I'll kick you out of here. I hope that's clear."

"Everyone is so *boring*."

Finn knocked my feet aside and sat on the sofa. He wore jeans, a gray Henley, and a belt. His brown hair was clean and recently cut. He had a scruff of beard, trimmed and neat. He looked fucking great. He always looked fucking great, and now he was healthy and happy and successful and in love. He pulled out his phone and tapped it.

"You offend me," I told him without any heat. I waved a towelled hand up and down. "All of this offends me."

"Yeah." He texted someone, his phone making that tapping sound.

"Why isn't your phone on silent?" I complained. "Are you a sociopath?"

"Shut up." Still texting.

"You have a great career and a hot girlfriend who loves you and a house and an apartment. You even have a dog. You are an acute reminder of my many shortcomings, Finn. At this particular moment, I don't need a reminder of how inadequate I am."

"You're not inadequate, Travis," Finn explained while texting. "You're actually talented. You're just dramatic, that's all."

I glared at him, uncomfortably reminded that Finn's dad had died of cancer a few years ago, and then Finn had been diagnosed with a brain tumor that had to be removed in surgery. He was healthy now, but he'd been through some shit, and yet he wasn't moping on a borrowed sofa, wishing he was high. Not like me. I wished—

I went still as something jarred loose in my mind. A hand tapping on the glass deep in my brain.

I looked at Katie onscreen again and thought, *I wish I was high*. On drugs. On her. On us. I wished I had her back here, that I had another chance. I wished I had the high of being a rock star again, of being someone that mattered. I wished I had so many highs.

That idea...sounded like a song.

Finn put his phone down. "Okay, that's done," he said. "You'll get a delivery in a few hours."

"A delivery of what?" For a second, I was so in my head that I wondered if Finn had told me about something and I had tuned it out.

"A keyboard," Finn said. "You need to be able to play while your hands get back in shape. You'll also get a laptop with software on it, headphones, and a mic."

I stared at him. "What? Why?"

"So you can write material and cut a demo. Something rough will do. I'm setting up a meeting with the Road Kings, and they're going to want to hear material before they agree to a deal."

I sat up. "Are you fucking kidding?"

"Not at all," Finn said. "If you want to stay in this apartment, you'll write something, record a demo, and go to the meeting. That's my condition."

I should have been mad. My rebellious, contrary side should have kicked up on cue, saying, *You can't tell me what to do. I don't take orders.* This was, by every metric, a great opportunity, one that I had shown no signs of deserving. I should be doing everything in my power to sink it.

And suddenly, I was so, so tired. I didn't want to be a useless lump on a borrowed sofa, complaining about his sore hands. I didn't want Finn to kick me out of here. I didn't want to disappoint my best friend. I didn't want to disappoint Katie.

In the deep recesses of my brain, some faint notes sounded. In sequence. The beginnings of a riff.

"Okay," I said to Finn.

He looked honestly surprised. "That's it? You'll do it?"

"Sure," I said, sadly amused at how certain he'd been that I would fuck this up. "Set up the meeting. But I'm just getting started. I need a little time to write."

"Of course." Finn shook his head. "I should have expected that you'd surprise me. Now, what's going on with Katie Armstrong? Because you followed her on Instagram."

"Oh, my god. You too?" I rolled my eyes.

"What? I figured out Instagram. Now spill. You didn't mention her when you stayed with me. What's happening?"

I told him. Sitting up with my aching hands in my lap, I gave him the whole sad story of my celibate week with Katie pretending to hook up, finishing with our agreed-on kiss at the airport as she left for L.A. Finn listened, and he didn't judge, because when he was a famous teenager he'd been set up with models. He'd been told at the time that he needed to date them for publicity. This was fucking with me at thirty-two, so I had no idea how it would screw with a teenager.

When I stopped talking, Finn didn't comment on my career or on Katie's. Instead, he said, "You like her."

"Everyone likes her," I said.

"Not everyone. *You* like her."

Shit. I slid down on the sofa again. "I feel all kinds of things about her," I mumbled.

"Name one thing," Finn said.

I gusted out a sigh. "I feel everything and nothing, all the time. I like her. I'll never have her. I'll take what I can get of her. I'd like to be better, but I don't believe I can. I want to go for it, but I'm sure I'll let her down. She's magic, but she can't fix me. Also, she's hot. I thought my dick was dead."

Finn's eyes widened as I made this speech. "Travis, you might need therapy."

"I tried that. The guy talked to me for ten minutes, then tried to sell me ketamine."

"Okay, that's...illegal?"

I shrugged.

"Well, then." Finn stood. "You'll have to do what every heartsick guy has done since the beginning of time. Write some songs about the girl you like."

FIFTEEN

Katie

"YOU DIDN'T SCREW TRAVIS WHITE," my agent said. "You were with him a whole week, and you didn't get him naked."

We were on a walk in Griffith Park—Stella's idea. This wasn't a leisurely, enjoyable walk, but a power walk of the burning-calories kind. Stella wore a snug workout top and skin-tight bike shorts that showed off her toned glutes. Her red hair was neatly slicked back in a ponytail. I panted alongside her in running shorts and a tee, my damp hair tangled, sunscreen sweating off my face. I was positive I was swallowing copious amounts of L.A. smog. I reminded myself to never again trust my agent's idea of "fun."

"I got him *so* naked," I argued. "I'm orgasmed out."

She gave me a sharp look from behind her sport sunglasses. "You forget that I was in on this from the beginning. Also, I know you. You don't date. You should, but you don't. You haven't dated since Jeremy, and you weren't orgasmed out when you dated him."

I winced. Jeremy was the year-long relationship. "Travis isn't Jeremy."

"He sure fucking isn't," Stella said. "Thank God. Jeremy didn't deserve you."

I was silent, taking this in. It was the nicest thing Stella had ever said to me, and it made my heart mushy.

"Anyway," Stella added. "It's been too long. Get Travis's dick in you, stat."

The mushy feeling drained away. I cleared my throat. "Um."

"You kissed him, at least," Stella went on, her arms pumping professionally as a couple of rollerbladers whizzed by. "I saw the goodbye at the airport. Nicely done. I could tell it wasn't the first time you'd kissed him. But you have to *sell* this, Katie. You aren't supposed to be dating a sweet guy. You're supposed to be boning the bad boy, day and night. I need to look at you two and *believe* it."

When we'd come up with this plan—even when I arrived in Portland and threw myself on Travis—I'd agreed with this. Now, it made me queasy. I didn't like Travis described as a *bad boy* as if there was nothing else to him. I didn't like hearing him talked about like a piece of meat. If the roles were reversed and Travis was a woman, it would be wrong to objectify him. I hated it.

To tell the truth, I didn't want to be here. Not in this park, getting lung cancer and listening to Stella talk about my sex life. Not in L.A. at all, in my weird white apartment with a closet full of clothes I didn't want to wear. I didn't want to do promo shoots or go to the cocktail party I'd been invited to tonight. I didn't want to call the personal trainer I'd been neglecting to book and set up sessions. I didn't want to wonder whether everyone who saw me onscreen thought I was getting Botox, or should get Botox, or should stop getting Botox. I didn't want to ponder lip fillers, cheek fillers, or bladed eyebrows. I didn't want to think about any of it.

I wanted to be curled up on that comfortable sofa in Portland, under a blanket with Travis, reading a book with the rain coming down the windows, lazily talking about what to have for dinner. I'd lived that life for a week. I hadn't thought about work. I hadn't worried. I had just existed, because Travis made it easy.

I had thought I was eager to get back into the game. No one can sit around forever, right? Chop chop, time to get going. Big plans. Now I found myself counting the sweaty minutes before I could book another flight and get out of here again.

Travis and I hadn't talked about when we'd meet again. What if he didn't want to see me? Well, he had to see me. It was part of the plan.

"I'm going back to Portland as soon as I can," I said to Stella.

"Get him to come here," she shot back. "You two should be seen in some L.A. hotspots. It would make the exposure happen faster." Her Apple watch beeped, and she glanced at it. "It's time for an official statement. I've put in a call to some PR people. We'll handle this the right way for maximum effect."

"No," I said.

Stella gave me a curious look. "Katie?"

"No," I said again. We were rounding the bend of our final lap, and I put on speed, anticipating my glorious return to my air conditioned car. "No to PR people. No to handling. No to all of it."

"But Edger Pinsent—"

"Is going to know a made-up PR romance when he sees

one," I interrupted her. "He's going to see it for what it is, because he's in this business. He's going to think it's lame."

Stella's arms pumped harder with annoyance as she processed this. "Fine," she finally said. "Can I at least send you the thriller script that came in? Can I do that much?"

I perked up in surprise. "A thriller?"

She nodded. "They called right after someone posted a photo of you and Travis taking a walk. The exec said that they hadn't considered you before, but the way you looked in that photo was exactly right for the part."

I bit back my smile. Travis's sexy, just-got-out-of-bed look had gotten me a call for a type of movie I'd never been offered before. He was going to be so pleased. "I'd love to do a thriller."

"It isn't an artsy indie film, but it would give your image some edge," Stella agreed. "They're looking to start shooting as soon as the casting is nailed down because someone just backed out with a scheduling conflict. They have everything ready to go."

"Send it to me," I told her. "I'll read it."

"Well," she sniffed. "At least I've been some use today."

I FACETIMED Travis as I was getting ready to go out. Gwen had just left after helping me with my hair and makeup. I hired a stylist for big events like a premiere, but since this was only a cocktail party, I usually did my hair and makeup myself. Gwen had insisted on helping me tonight after she dropped off the dress she'd ordered.

Travis picked up right away. He was on the sofa in the Portland apartment, wearing a faded Aerosmith T-shirt. His hair was wet. "Hey," he said, his expression brightening as he saw me. "Jesus, you look beautiful."

"Oh." I patted my hair self-consciously. Why did a compliment sound different coming from him? "Thank you."

Silence descended for a moment as we looked at each other through the screen.

"What is it?" I finally asked.

"You look beautiful," Travis said again.

I laughed. "Okay. Thank you, again. Did you just get out of the shower?" Showers had been delicately negotiated during the week we were together, since the apartment had only one bathroom. There was careful choreographing of one person in the living room while the other showered, so there would be no chance of seeing each other naked. If my movies were a little raunchier, I thought that would be a funny scene—the bump-into-each-other-naked scene. I made a mental note.

Travis shook his head. "I went running," he admitted. "It's raining out."

"You went for a run in the cold, dark rain?" He had never gone running—or worked out any other way—in our week. He hadn't even mentioned it.

He ran a hand through his hair, looking embarrassed. I had a sudden rush of memory of how good he smelled, like men's deodorant and warm male skin. I wished I could crawl through the screen.

"I thought going for a run would wake up my creativity," Travis said. "You know, jolt my brain into action. I don't know if it worked. All I feel now is cold."

Creativity? I gasped in a breath. "You're writing music?"

"I am *trying* to write music," he corrected me. "Specifically, I'm flogging my exhausted, out-of-shape brain into expressing itself in a way that isn't completely self-pitying or self-destructive. The results are inconclusive as of yet."

"You're writing music." I clapped my hands in excitement.

He shook his head, but a smile touched the corners of his

mouth. "You wouldn't be clapping if you heard what I've come up with so far."

"My favorite Seven Dog Down song is 'Four in the Morning,'" I said. "It's sweet and a little sad, and your voice is so sexy in it."

His eyebrows shot up. "Is it?"

I had said it without thinking, but I wasn't embarrassed. "Yes it is, and you know it. If you wrote an album of songs that sounded like that one, I would buy it a thousand times over."

His gaze had dropped down to my shoulders, where the spaghetti straps of my dress were visible in the frame. "I want to see your dress," he said.

So I propped up my phone, then stood back so he could see all of it. It was a black knee-length cocktail dress, and the loose skirt had a light layer of tulle. It looked classy and flirty and—I thought—sexy at the same time.

I twirled, and Travis cleared his throat. "Yeah. Beautiful."

"One of the production companies that produces my movies is throwing a cocktail party," I explained. "I'm not looking forward to it, but I have to go."

"Why don't you want to go?"

"It's boring. These events are networking events for the producers. The actors are invited to be stared at and to get our pictures taken. It makes me feel a bit like a dancing bear in a circus. Plus, I have to stand around awkwardly without a date."

"That's my job," Travis protested. "I would have come to L.A. to go with you."

I shook my head. "We're not official yet. But once we are, you'll be stuck going to these events with me, I'm afraid."

"I don't mind." Of course he didn't mind, because he would have gone to events with Sabrina Lowe. Though I didn't remember seeing them out much together. It would be nice to have a boyfriend again to go to events with, even if it was a fake boyfriend. It really sucked going to these things alone.

"When are we official?" Travis asked. "How does that work?"

"We announce it on Instagram."

"And when is that?"

"Whenever we decide is good. Wait a minute," I said as a thought came to me. I walked closer to my phone again. "Do you own a suit?"

Travis shrugged. "Most of them were repossessed." He grabbed a blanket from the back of the sofa and tucked it around him, making me sad when the tattoos on his arms disappeared.

"Send me your measurements," I told him. "I'll get my assistant Gwen and my stylist on it. We'll get you suited up for events."

"No way. I can get some good threads. Don't worry about it."

I couldn't remember hearing anyone use the word *threads* in honest conversation, and I didn't know why I thought it was charming. I was starting to suspect I had a crush on this man. "How do you plan to get designer clothes?"

"I know people. I'll figure it out."

Figuring things out on the fly seemed to be the way he lived life, which was the opposite of my approach. I was distracted from the thought when he ran a hand through his hair and I noticed the red welts on his fingertips. "What happened to your hand?"

He flexed his hand and looked at it, as if he'd forgotten. "Guitar," he explained. "I'll toughen up."

He'd been playing guitar. It was crazy that I was about to go to a ritzy Hollywood cocktail party, and Travis was chilly and alone in a rainy apartment writing songs, and I would have given a lot of money to be where he was in that moment instead of where I was. I didn't want to make nice with producers. I wanted to watch movies with Travis and hear him play music—anything at all.

"I'm almost done with my obligations here," I said. "Then I'm coming back to Portland."

He blinked his gorgeous blue eyes at the change of topic and seemed to sit up straighter. "Yeah? When?"

I calculated how quickly I could get out of town. "A few days."

He smiled, one of his real smiles that made my insides melt. "Damn. I guess I'm getting kicked out of bed again."

I stared at him, and all I wanted to say was, *Then don't leave the bed this time. Stay in it with me.* Because I didn't want to just watch movies with Travis, or just listen to him play music. I wanted to do a lot more than that.

Did he? He'd made an offer when we first met, but not since I turned him down—actually, after I told him to *fuck off*. Yeah, he might have gotten the message not to try again.

I tried to stay businesslike. "I think we should do our announcement once I'm back in Portland. That's the best timing."

"Okay," he said.

"It won't be through a PR company, just something you and I agree on together. A soft launch."

Travis waggled his eyebrows. "When's the hard launch? That's what I'm interested in."

It was like he was reading my mind, and suddenly I was awkward and mute, like a kid at her first middle-school dance. I should have something witty and seductive at the tip of my tongue. I was thirty-four years old, for God's sake. I should be able to think of *something*.

But I had nothing. I sat silent for a moment too long, and Travis held up a hand, showing me his guitar injuries again.

"Forget I said that, sorry," he said.

"No, wait."

"I made it weird."

"You didn't."

"Katie, it's—"

"Look, I meant—"

"We should—"

"Go to your event." His voice was gentle. "Try to have fun. Send me your flight information when you have it. I'll see you when you get here."

SIXTEEN

Travis

Katie: Landing in twenty minutes.

Travis: I'm here. Just parked. I'll come to Arrivals.

Katie: I think you should kiss me hello.

Travis: Okay.

Katie: It would be realistic. Right?

Travis: I'll do it. How would you rate the last one?

Katie: Perfect. 10/10, no notes.

Travis: Good to know. I'll do that again.

Katie: Lucky for you, I always travel with mints in my purse.

Travis: I'm not worried, babe.

Katie: Also, I'm not wearing lipstick. We should probably discuss lipstick at some point. And lip gloss. Does either bother you? I have setting spray I use on set, but it smells weird. Or I could just not wear it.

Travis: Wear whatever makes you happy. Lipstick doesn't scare me.

Katie: It could be a problem, depending on how much public kissing we plan to do. It's a worse problem if any tongue is involved.

Travis: Are you requesting tongue for this airport kiss? I need a heads up for that.

Katie: Forget I mentioned it. Let's stick to the plan.

I ROLLED my shoulders as I walked into the arrivals hall. I needed to focus. Katie had forgiven me for coming onto her *again*, and she'd given me another chance to do this right. She'd asked me to kiss her. I didn't want to screw this up.

I got double takes as I walked through the airport crowd, and I heard murmurs. Portland was a chill place, I knew now, full of people who didn't go nuts over celebrities. I did the walk that worked best in public—a rolling saunter with some speed to it, gaze straight ahead, posture relaxed, a way of moving that said *I'm the cool dude you think I am, I'm not stuck up, but right now I'm on my way somewhere.* You had to walk the line between businesslike and unfriendly. It helped that I wore a hoodie and a baseball cap, so a lot of people missed recognizing me.

While I waited at the arrival doors, a few people made eye contact with me and gave me smiles or nods. I nodded back, then focused on the doors, making it clear I was expecting someone.

When Katie came through the doors with her rolling bag, I waited for her to notice me. Then I zeroed in on her, strode up to her, cupped her face in my hands, and kissed her.

I didn't open her lips, but I kissed her more deeply than I had when she left. I kissed her like I'd been thinking about her nonstop, like I'd been restless waiting for her to come back. I kissed her as if I'd like to be polite in public, but at the sight of her I just couldn't fucking do it. Like at the sight of her, I'd forgotten all of my good intentions.

Her cheeks were flushed when I pulled away, and a strangled word came out of her throat. "Oh."

"I'm obsessed, remember?" I took the handle of her bag in one hand and flung my other arm over her shoulders, tugging her into my side. "You're a sex goddess. You're only back in Portland because I've been begging you nonstop, and you finally took pity on me."

"Right." Her arm slid around my waist as we walked through the crowd toward the doors. People gawked openly at us. "I think we gave them a show," she said in a low voice.

"That's the idea." I led her out toward the parking lot and my car. She felt good under my arm, her hand curled against my hipbone and her arm snug against my lower back. A guy hauling a suitcase from the back of a cab gave me a thumbs up, and I winked back at him.

The rich, famous rock star, getting the girl and taking her home. Another day in paradise.

KATIE TOOK A LONG, hot shower when we got to the apartment. She came out of the bathroom wearing navy sweatpants and a T-shirt, her hair damp around her shoulders. I forced my gaze away from her shirt, but not before I noted that yes, she was wearing something under it. *Nice try at being a gentleman, bro. Try again.*

If she noticed my wandering eyeballs, she didn't let on. She put a laptop bag on the counter and slid her laptop out. "I'm starving," she said. "Are we going out?"

"Nope." I poured myself ice water from the pitcher in the fridge, which I had stocked for her. I'd taken note of what she liked to eat the last time she was here. "That isn't in the script."

"It isn't?"

I gave her a look as I sipped my water, trying not to remember how her lips had tasted. Good. They'd tasted good. "Babe, it's been almost two weeks. I've been dying. It was the best sex I ever had, and my balls are bluer than the Mediterranean. Please tell me we're having reunion sex for at least a few hours. Put me out of my misery."

Her cheeks flamed red. "Right. I suppose we would do that."

"I'm just telling it like it is. Or like it would be. You know what I mean."

She lifted her hair from her neck and blew out a breath. "You make a good point. I didn't want to go out, anyway. We'll order in." She looked around the room, caught sight of my guitar, and whirled back to me. "Play me the music you've been working on."

I groaned. "Katie, no. A sex goddess does *not* listen to her boyfriend's terrible music and pretend she likes it to feed his ego. It's beneath her."

"She does if her boyfriend is Travis White," Katie argued.

"Dubious claims of my talent aside, still no."

"You *are* talented. I'm sure the music is good. I'm dying to hear it."

"Later. What's that?" I pointed to a thick stack of pages resting on top of her laptop.

She picked up the stack, playing along with the change of subject for the moment. "This is the thriller script I've been offered. I think I'm going to take it."

"A thriller? That's new."

"It's new, it's dark, it's different, and they offered it to me because they saw me with you."

I blinked. As much effort as I'd put into this fake-dating thing, I hadn't thought much about it actually *working*. "Really?"

"Really." Her cheeks were still pink, this time with excitement. "They saw a picture of me walking around Portland with my hot boyfriend and my sex hair, and they decided I'd be perfect for the role."

Our gazes locked. I was happy for her. I wanted to kiss her again.

Actually, I wanted to scoop her up and put her ass on the counter. Then I wanted to tug down her sweatpants, get on my knees, and—

This was agony, wanting this. And yet I couldn't stomach the thought of being anywhere else than right here.

"You're welcome," I managed to say.

Katie smiled and held the pages out to me. "Would you read it and tell me what you think?"

I took the script reluctantly. "I'm not in the movie business."

"Still, before I decide, I want your opinion."

Who the hell wanted my opinion on a script? I was hardly

Edgar Pinsent. But I was curious about what might be Katie's next project. "You don't know anything about my taste in movies," I warned her.

"I know you like mine."

"I do," I admitted. "I was only a little bit stoned." I didn't tell her about my crying session in front of *The Christmas Date*. If I could hold on to the thinnest shred of my male dignity, I would keep it.

"I've been told my movies go well with weed," Katie said Fuck, I liked her. "I'd appreciate if you'd read this script *sans* cannabis, if you would."

"I'm happy to oblige."

We smiled at each other for too long, and then the air got heavy, and it was hard to shut out the fact that we were alone in this apartment with no distractions. And we had kissed at the airport. And it would be night in a few hours.

"Oh, shit," I said, jolting us out of the moment. I put the script down. "I forgot to clear out the bedroom for you." I'd slept in until it was almost time to pick her up. I had been up late recording the demo for the Road Kings.

As I climbed the loft stairs to the bedroom, I heard Katie's footsteps behind me. "Wait, Travis," she said.

"This won't take long." Was my underwear on the floor of the bedroom? The odds were good. Did Katie care about underwear? Were we past that by now? I had no idea, because this fake relationship was confusing as hell. "I can launder the sheets," I told her as I swept into the room. "Not that I did anything gross in the bed. I don't even jerk off, honestly. The last year has been weird."

"Travis," she said again.

"Ah, shit. I made it awkward again." I scooped up my underwear which, yes, was on the floor. "Sorry, Katie. I swear I'm not—"

"You don't need to move out of the bedroom."

I straightened and looked at her, my boxer briefs crumpled in my hand. "No way. I'm not making you take the sofa. Forget it."

She looked frustrated. "I'm saying that we can share."

In the moment of shocked silence, I felt a rush of heat all over my body that was almost embarrassing. Share a bed with Katie? *Yes.* My brain screamed it at top volume. *Absolutely fucking yes.*

"What do you mean?" I asked her, because I couldn't trust myself in that moment.

"I mean that it's silly for you to sleep on the sofa," she replied. "We don't need to pretend like we're in a 1960s sitcom. We're going to be rooming together for a while, and we're both adults. I think we can get along."

That only added to the confusion. Did she mean *get along* with my dick inside her and a string of stellar orgasms? Maybe she meant *get along* as in oral only? Also good. Or she might mean *get along* as in we fall asleep fully clothed every night, like mature adults who don't think about fucking all the time.

That last one, apparently, was not me.

It didn't matter what she meant by *get along*, really, because I would take any one of those three options over sleeping alone.

Be cool, Travis. Be cool.

I nodded. "Ah, yeah," I said, sounding like a fifteen-year-old doofus whose crush just asked him out. Real smooth. "I can see—yeah. That makes sense. We can share." I realized I was still holding my underwear, so I turned and threw it onto the pile of laundry in the hamper. "No sweat," I said.

A smirk touched her pretty lips. "No sweat. Unless you snore."

"I'm a cone of silence," I said.

"Good. So am I. I like to keep the ceiling fan on." She held up a finger. "I must have one leg out from under the covers, no more and no less, or I can't sleep."

"One leg," I said. "Got it." I was barely listening. I was too busy computing whether this meant I was supposed to make a move. Would making a move screw this up? Would *not* making a move screw this up?

Why was this so hard? I was a fucking rock star. You meet a woman, you make a move, she always says yes. Done.

I never had any idea what I was doing with Katie.

And still, I didn't miss that old life at all.

SEVENTEEN

Katie

I TRIED TO REGRET IT. Honestly, I did. I tried to second guess myself and freak out, tried to have my usual good-girl reaction to anything that might go wrong. I tried to be embarrassed, and just like when I'd jumped him and kissed him the first day, I wasn't. I only felt giddy.

I was *in bed*. With Travis White.

In. Bed.

Granted, he was on his side of the bed, and I was on mine. We were both clothed—me in my pajama shorts and top, him in a pair of loose plaid flannel sleep pants and a white tank top that showed his hot-as-hell tattoos. We were on top of the covers, propped up on pillows against the headboard. We were not touching. But it was night outside, and we were alone in bed together.

In. Bed.

This was much different than when he slept downstairs. I

was close enough to notice new details about him—sleep details. His bare feet were flawless, not ugly and weird like some men's were. No. Of course Travis had feet that could have been carved by Michelangelo. The lamplight made his skin glow even more golden than usual. He sprawled easily with my script propped on his bent knees, turning the pages as he read. He was truly gorgeous, and after two weeks away from him, it hit me all over again.

He sensed me staring, and he glanced at me. "I'm almost done," he said. "Be patient."

I nodded, letting him think that I was leering over him because I was eager about the script, not because at this proximity I could get tantalizing whiffs of his skin. Not because I was thinking dirty thoughts I'd never thought about any man before, like imagining running my tongue along the perfect line of his collarbone.

Right, the script. It was called *Honor Student*, and it was about a high school teacher—me—who becomes convinced that one of her teenaged students is a serial killer. The story follows her life unraveling as she becomes more and more obsessed with the student, following him around and looking in his windows, never leaving him alone. Murders are happening, and she's convinced this seventeen-year-old kid is a killer. It was a dark story, twisted and unsettling, completely out of character for me. I thought it was amazing, and I couldn't wait to play her.

Travis turned the last page and flung the script onto the bed. "Holy shit," he said. "That ending."

"Good, right?" I said.

He shook his head. "I didn't see that twist coming at all. But it's all there in the previous scenes when you think about it. It was set up the whole time. What a mindfuck."

"A good mindfuck?"

"A very good mindfuck." He handed the script back to me. "You should do it."

"You think I can?"

"I think you'd ace it. Seeing you play that part is going to blow people's minds. It's going to blow Edgar Pinsent's mind."

"That's the idea," I said, though to be honest, I hadn't thought about Edgar Pinsent when I read the script. I had just thought it was an amazing story. "If you like it, I'm going to take it. They want to shoot in L.A. next month. I'll have to go back for script meetings and prep."

Travis nodded. "All right."

"Are you planning to stay in Portland?"

"For a while." He scratched the back of his neck, and I watched in fascination as his arm moved, the tattoos flashing out of my line of vision. "It depends on how tomorrow goes. Which reminds me, you're going to be on your own for a few hours tomorrow. I have a meeting at the Road Kings' studio to talk about a record deal."

My jaw dropped open. "You're going to a meeting about a record deal? That's amazing."

"I'm dreading it," he admitted. "I talked a lot of shit about the Road Kings when my band was on top. I was a cocky asshole, and now I pretty much have to ask them to give me a chance. My ego isn't happy about it."

It was such a vulnerable thing to admit. Unexpected. I liked cocky Travis, but I liked Travis in a reflective mood even more. I moved closer to him and sat with my legs crossed, facing him. "Just tell them you've changed," I offered. "Tell them you're sorry."

Travis rolled his eyes. "I can't do that, obviously."

"Why not?"

"They'll think I'm weak."

"If you don't, they'll think you're a jerk."

"Better a jerk than a doormat. I have to act like I don't care whether they want to do this or not. It's the only way."

I sighed in frustration. "Why are men?"

"I don't know. I'll just tough it out. Either they'll like the music or they won't. If they do, I'll stay here for a few months to record an album. But it'll be easy to go to L.A. whenever you need me. No more parties by yourself. Our deal is still on."

The deal. Right. I picked up my phone—I had spent my time scrolling while Travis read the script—and swiped it awake. "We were noticed at the airport," I told him. "Check it out." I opened Instagram and turned my phone for him to see.

He touched the phone and pulled it closer so we were both holding it. I watched his blue eyes focus on the photo a fan had taken of him and me. Travis was kissing me, his arm around my waist, me on my toes with my head tilted back. We looked like a couple in a movie, but better. I had never looked so easy, so confident, so in the moment in any of my movies. I looked like I had been swept up by the man of my dreams after being apart from him for too long.

Travis was quiet as he looked at the photo. I wondered what he was thinking.

"I swear I don't scour the internet looking for mentions of myself," I said. "My assistant sent this to me, and she only sends me the good things. You can read the comments. There are hundreds."

Travis shook his head. "No thanks."

"They're nice comments," I assured him. "People love us together. They say that they would never have put you and me together, but somehow it works. They say that we look good. That you look good. Which you do." My cheeks burned hot, but I pressed on. "I think you look really good, Travis. All the time."

His gaze rose to mine, and I locked into that stunning blue, unable to look away. He was so much like clear glass in that moment—I could see uncertainty, curiosity, attraction. And yet there was so much I didn't know. We'd muddled this so-called relationship so much that I couldn't read his intentions, and maybe he couldn't read mine. That suddenly felt tragic. I'd kissed him the first time because I'd been reminded that life was short. Why had I forgotten again?

"It was a nice kiss," he said softly, still holding my gaze.

My pulse leapt. I didn't know which kiss he was talking about. It didn't matter.

"It was a perfect kiss," I whispered back. I reached up and brushed my fingers over his jaw, his cheekbone.

The attraction in his eyes flared, then darkened. He'd been waiting for this. He'd been feeling it. He wasn't immune.

I thought he might say something else, but he didn't. He leaned toward me, cupped my jaw, and kissed me.

It started slow, exploring, and then his tongue parted my lips. My phone dropped to the bed with a soft sound. We wound around each other, warm and sure, and in a moment I straddled his lap, my hands in his hair as his palms slid under my shirt and up my bare back. How did he taste so good, so satisfying? I relished the tang of his flavor, the feel of his lean body against mine. His hands explored my skin under my shirt, memorizing the contours of my ribcage, the dip of my spine, my waist.

His hair was soft in my grip, the strands brushing the backs of my hands. I broke the kiss.

"Katie," he said softly.

In reply, I let go of his hair and lifted the hem of his shirt. Travis raised his arms and let me pull it off, dropping it to the bed. A thin silver necklace adorned his collarbone, cool against his golden skin. His tattoo ink was dark against his biceps, elegant flames licking up the curve of his right shoulder, and I had the urge to sink my teeth into that spot.

His warm hands pushed my shirt up, too, and then it joined his on the bed and I was bare from the waist up. And then we were kissing again, more urgently, as if we couldn't get enough. His touch was dirty and respectful at the same time, wandering my bare skin with open desire without grabbing or squeezing. His shoulders were sleek and strong, the muscles sliding under his skin. His palms cupped my breasts, and all I could think was, *the hottest man I've ever met is touching me,* and I still didn't panic, even though the lamplight next to the bed illuminated everything in its soft glow. This had never happened before. I always worried about something on my body in these moments, and I'd never had sex with a man I found half as hot as Travis. Why wasn't I freaking out?

When he briefly broke the kiss, I said, "We probably shouldn't do this."

His reply was confident. "We should definitely do this." His hands learned the shapes of my breasts, making my breath leave my body. "This is the only thing we should be doing." His hands paused. "Unless you want me to stop?"

"I was giving you an out."

"I've been thinking about this for weeks," Travis said. "I don't want an out."

We kissed some more, and he turned us so I was on my back on the bed. My head landed on the script, abandoned on the bedspread, and the paper made a crinkling sound. Travis put the script on the bedside table, and as he reached, his body stretched gracefully across the bed, I slid my hands down his flat stomach and under the elastic waist of his sleep pants.

He groaned softly, and the sound combined with the heated flush on his skin as I gripped him made me crazy. When I moved my palm over him, he pressed his weight into his elbows and shifted his hips. I had never experienced anything so sexy in my life. Why hadn't we done this the first minute we met? What were we thinking?

No, the problem wasn't him. It was me. Travis had offered this when we met at the basketball game the first night. Had I actually told him no? Why? I needed my head examined.

He kissed me deeply, his hips doing that magical move that shifted him in my grip. "We need condoms," I gasped when we broke apart.

"Bedside drawer." At my look of hazy surprise, he gave me a rock star grin. "I bought them yesterday. I'm an optimistic guy."

"A deluded guy," I shot back without thinking, and then we both laughed softly because he was so obviously *not* deluded. He kissed me again, and I felt the tickle of the silver chain around his neck dragging against my skin, and somehow that turned me on even more.

His lips left mine to travel down my neck, then to my breasts. The shift in position put him out of my hand's reach. His palms slid down the curve of my waist. I reached for the bedside drawer and opened it, rummaging blindly inside.

"Not yet," Travis said, lifting his mouth from the side of my breast. "I'm going to last about forty-five seconds. I have work to do first."

My head spun at those words, and then his hands tugged at the waist of my sleep shorts, and I finally panicked. "Wait."

Travis stopped. He paused kissing the skin just under my belly button and lifted his head, fixing his blue eyes on me.

"What is it?" he asked.

"I, um…" Oh, god, he was so gorgeous. "I don't—" I pointed down my body. "I don't wax."

He blinked. "You don't—What?"

"I don't wax," I admitted. *Everyone* in Hollywood waxed. It was the norm. No one in Hollywood had seen pubic hair in fifteen years. "I haven't been dating, and I don't do nude scenes, and I don't do bathing suit or underwear scenes." I was talking and I couldn't stop. "I know it's weird, right? I kept putting it off. Honestly, those women at the waxing places are terrifying, even when they're trying to be nice. I always think they're judging me. Besides which, it really hurts, and I feel like no one talks about that. If I thought someone would see, I would have made an appointment, but—"

"Katie." Travis's voice was rough but patient. His gaze was still fixed on me. "I'm about to enter paradise, and you think I'm worried about waxing?"

"Everyone waxes!" I argued. "I just think I should warn you that if you keep going, you'll time travel to 1990."

"If your pussy is in 1990," he explained slowly, "then that's where I want to go."

Our gazes locked in silence.

"Are you done?" he asked finally. "Because if you're finished freaking out, I'd like to go down on you now."

"Yeah, I'm done," I breathed. His hands curled into my waistband and tugged it down. I lay back, looking up at the ceiling, my heart pounding. Travis slid off my shorts and panties, and then he gently pressed my thighs open, and then everything went away.

Everything.

In my experience, oral sex could be fun, but it was also awkward. No one should see me quite so up close in an area I couldn't see myself. Besides which, every man I'd ever been with *thought* he was good at it, and every one had been wrong, even the well-meaning ones.

Travis White was a genius.

I forgot where I was, and then I forgot my own name. Time had no meaning. It could have been hours or years, but it was more likely minutes before I was a puddle of hot wax who would do anything, say anything if only he would keep going. How did he know that exact spot? Was he bending my knees?

The orgasm that hit me was so intense I twisted on the bed. I heard my phone fall off the mattress to the floor with a thud. Travis lifted his mouth off of me, and he'd barely shifted his weight and reached for a condom when I rolled him to his back and straddled his lap, kissing him. Tasting myself.

His back hit the headboard as he lifted his hips underneath me. He slid his pants down and put on the condom, and I lowered onto him with a groan as his hands gripped my hips.

I had never done this before, never jumped on a man and ridden him as if I couldn't stand it if he wasn't inside me. I braced my hands on the headboard and Travis moved with me in perfect rhythm, both of us wordless now, sweat slicking between us, his fingers digging into my hips. He pressed his forehead into the side of my neck and I felt him pulse inside the condom as he sighed against my skin. When I touched his neck, I felt his blood pounding, and the beat seemed as frantic as mine.

He inhaled a breath. "I knew that would be so fucking good," he rasped.

I was shaking and exultant and terrified. I felt powerful, and at the same time I felt like my skin had been stripped raw. I felt like I had been pulled apart and left in naked, vulnerable pieces.

"Katie?" Travis asked, lifting his head. "You all right?"

"Yeah," I breathed.

His hands left my hips and his arms came around me, squeezing gently. "Look at me," he said.

I did as he told me, locking my gaze onto those blue, blue eyes. This was Travis. Familiar and beautiful, his hair mussed and his skin still flushed with sex. I felt a familiar warmth at the sight of him, a thrill of pleasure, even now.

"Hi," he said.

"Hi," I said back, marveling at him. Because he'd done it— he'd made me feel as giddy as if we'd just met. He was flirting with me even now, naked and tangled together in bed. I felt myself beaming at him, unable to help it.

I was in big, big trouble.

And somehow, I didn't care.

EIGHTEEN

Travis

SITTING in the driver's seat of my parked car, I pulled out my phone and texted Finn.

> Me: I have good news. Important news. My dick isn't broken.

> Finn: ???

> Finn: Oh, I get it. Katie Armstrong?

> Me: Right on, my man. You guessed it. It turns out I can still jive.

> Finn: That's good news, I guess? Congratulations. I think.

> Me: With Katie, things just started flowing again. If you know what I mean.

> Finn: Okay.

> Me: It was spectacular. I could write poetry for days. I might start working out.

> Finn: I got the picture.

> Me: You should see her naked. Incredible.

> Finn: Please stop.

I grinned at my phone, because making Finn uncomfortable had been one of my favorite hobbies for years. I meant what I said, though. Katie naked *was* incredible. And I *could* still jive.

The phone rang in my hand. Finn. I answered it. "Oh, hey man, what's up? I haven't heard from you in a while."

"Travis," he said, "aren't you supposed to be meeting with the Road Kings?"

I adjusted the baseball cap on my head. "Is that today?"

"It's right now."

"Oh, man," I said. "What time is it?"

There was a pause, and then he said, "You're already there, aren't you?"

I squinted through the windshield at the RKS studio, which I was parked in front of at eleven o'clock in the morning, because rock stars never had nine a.m. meetings. "Send me the address. I'll try and make it."

He sighed. "Are you going to spend all day screwing with me, or are you going to go to the meeting?"

"I know which one is more fun."

"Travis—"

"Okay, okay. Jeez. I'm here. I might be talking to you so that I can delay going inside. But only for a few minutes. I'll go."

"It's going to be great," Finn said. "They're nice guys."

I was sure they were nice to Finn. Me, not so much. "If they tell me to go fuck myself, it isn't because I didn't show up. I just want the record to show that. It'll be because they hate me, and also because of the music."

Finn's voice was annoyed. "I haven't heard the music, because you refused to send it to me."

"It sucks," I said. "I'm a fraud. Remember how I was the lead singer of a band, and they wouldn't let us write any of the music? Remember how all I had to do was show up and sing because I wasn't good enough to do anything else? I do."

"You're talented," Finn said.

I had actually believed that for a big part of my life, but now, sitting in this parking lot, I was absolutely convinced of the opposite. Which was funny, because in the years I *wasn't* famous, I was sure I was good. It was being in one of the world's most successful bands that made me feel worthless. How did that make sense?

I frowned, because that idea sounded like something I could use in a song.

"Travis?" Finn said. "I said you're talented. Now go into the meeting. Please."

"Fine, here goes," I said, and hung up. I adjusted my ball cap again and rolled my shoulders. *My dick works,* I reminded myself. It cheered me up. I got out of the car.

RKS was in Vancouver, over the border from Portland, in Washington. It was a blocky building in an industrial park with only a stencilled sign on the glass door indicating that rock stars worked here. There were a half dozen other cars in the parking lot. A chill wind blew, and I zipped up my hoodie and pulled the hood over my ball cap. If I could have pulled the hood all the way over my face for this meeting, I would have.

I had refused to dress up. Jeans, Chucks, and a sweatshirt were what the Road Kings would get. If I wore anything else, they'd think it was weird, like I was trying to impress them. I was *not* trying to impress them, even though I was.

The door opened, and a woman stood there, smiling and waving at me. I had a crazy moment when I recognized her but I couldn't place her face, and then I had it. I felt myself smiling in pleasure as I came toward her.

"Sienna, hi," I said.

Sienna Maplethorpe was a music journalist. I'd met her years ago, when I was still in Seven Dog Down and she was just starting out. I'd given her an exclusive interview, which she'd sold to an online magazine. Sienna had shoulder-length dark hair, cool tortoiseshell glasses, and the best kind of music-chick vibe. She wore a stylish black dress and lace-up Docs, and when I came though the door, she hugged me as if we were old friends. "It's so good to see you!" she exclaimed.

I hugged her back hard, mostly because it was good to see a familiar, friendly face. She smelled great. Then I remembered that even though I was out of the loop, I did know some of the industry gossip, and Sienna was dating Stone Zeeland, the Road Kings' guitarist. Which meant that I was starting this meeting by hugging Stone Zeeland's girlfriend, and Stone Zeeland was six-four and terrifying.

I let Sienna go and stood politely back, looking around. We were in the studio lobby, and there was no one else here. "It's great to see you, too," I said. "I didn't know you would be here."

"I wouldn't miss it." Sienna clasped her hands together, as if trying not to clap. "New Travis White music? A solo album? It's the best news I've heard all year." She held up her hands. "Don't worry, this meeting is off the record. This is personal for me because I'm so excited to hear it."

"Okay," I said.

"But once the time comes, I *am* going to beg you for an exclusive. I give you fair warning. You won't be able to get rid of me until you say yes."

I shrugged. "No need for all that. I'll say yes now."

She smiled again, because she was actually excited. Were there people this excited to get music from me? Too late, I realized I should have sent Finn the music ahead of time. If it really was bad, he would have told me.

"Sienna, give me the truth," I said, nodding past her shoulder to the door we were about to go through. "How much do they hate me?"

"Not as much as they think they do," she said. "They've mellowed a bit."

"With age?" I raised my brows and grinned at her. The Road Kings were forty, and Sienna was closer to my age. Her rock star boyfriend was older than her.

She punched my shoulder. "With wisdom," she clarified. "Also, I've softened them up by telling them about how you're dating Katie Armstrong. Neal's wife and daughter both *love* Katie Armstrong. So do I."

I blinked. "You know about Katie?"

"I'm on Instagram, obviously," Sienna said. "It's part of the job for me. The guys hate social media, but their wives don't, and Neal's daughter is a teenager. I really want to ask you about Katie when I interview you. You two are adorable."

I rubbed my chin. "We are," I said, trying to sound casual and not like I'd explored Katie's naked body a few hours ago. "We are adorable."

"Okay, go in," Sienna said, taking my arm and pushing me toward the door. "I'll be in the back of the room, but I won't say anything unless there's blood. Then I'll fake an emergency phone call and get you out of the room."

"I owe you, babe," I said.

"I owe *you*," she replied. "You gave me my big break when I was no one. You didn't have to do that. I'll never forget it."

Had I done that? I actually had. I thought back to the day she'd interviewed me, the guy I'd been then. A big deal, a rock star, high on my own supply and on a couple of Adderall I'd taken that morning. What a douchebag that guy was. The profile Sienna had written had been nicer to me than it needed to be.

"I said yes to your pitch because I thought you were cool," I told her, which was the truth. She blinked and looked so happy, you'd think I'd written her a Shakespearean sonnet.

"Here goes nothing," I said, and walked through the door.

WE WERE MEETING in the studio's control room, which had a sofa and some chairs among the speakers and sound boards. "Everyone, this is Travis," Sienna said. She stood behind me and put her hands on my shoulders, which made Stone Zeeland glare at me. Great.

"Travis, this is Stone." Sienna gestured to Stone Zeeland, ignoring his dangerous glare. "That's Neal Watts." She indicated the band's bass player, a nice-looking guy with brown hair and a cool jacket. "That's Axel de Vries." She pointed to the drummer, a blond guy with tats on his arms who gave me a nod. "And Denver Gilchrist."

Denver Gilchrist, the lead singer of the Road Kings, the man I'd seen onstage when I was eighteen and decided I wanted to be. He was sitting on a chair that was turned backward, his forearms resting across the back. At forty, he still had his long, lean grace and his restless energy. He watched me with an unreadable look, and I could have sworn the corner of his mouth was trying not to smile.

Sienna directed my attention to a man I didn't know. "That's Will Hale," she explained. "He's the band's manager and the owner of the studio."

Will Hale was tall and clean-cut, wearing a crisp button-down shirt with the throat unbuttoned and an immaculate pair of dress pants. He was obviously the businessman of the group. He gave me a polite nod and explained, "I'm the one who knows how to work the sound system in here."

"Hi," I said. Sienna's hands on my shoulders directed me toward an empty chair, and I sat down.

We all looked at each other.

"So, um," I said to break the ice. "I'm sorry about the glitter bomb."

Neal Watts crossed his arms. "You're not sorry at all," he pointed out.

I raised my gaze to the ceiling. "Well, it was funny, so I'm not sorry about that. But it was also rude, so in the context of the rudeness, yeah, I'm sorry about that part."

"That's an interesting apology," Axel de Vries said. "It was ingenious, I'll give you that. Hiding a glitter bomb in a bottle of non-alcoholic champagne."

"It took weeks to set up," I said. "I put a lot of thought into it. It cost a lot of money, too, if that makes you feel any better."

"You put so much work into one prank," Neal said. Stone was still glaring. Denver was watching calmly, quiet.

I lowered my gaze to look at them. "You guys were shit-talking my band," I explained. "I couldn't resist." I remembered I was supposed to be apologizing. "In hindsight, you guys were right. We weren't a very good band. I didn't have much impulse control back then."

"And you do now?"

This was Denver. I pushed down the voice in my head screaming that Denver Gilchrist was talking to me and tried to look unbothered. "I'm improving myself," I told him.

Stone Zeeland leaned forward in his seat on the sofa and leaned his elbows on his knees. "Enough small talk," he said in a gruff voice, and I tried not to remember how incredibly fucking good he was at guitar, how he made it sing onstage and in every Road Kings record, while I'd had to wrap my hands in tea towels and cry on a sofa after an hour of playing. "You've got some music for us to hear, but before we listen, here's the deal. You might be a shit, but you also got fucked over by your record company, and that's not what we do. We made our own studio and our own company so that we wouldn't get fucked over anymore and so that other artists wouldn't get fucked over, either."

"Okay," I said, "but to be honest, that's hard to believe."

Will Hale cleared his throat. Denver smiled at me for the first time.

"You don't believe it because you know the music business," he said. "If we work with you, we make the best record possible, we promote it, we get you on the road to promote it. But we don't own you. We do things differently here."

I shrugged. "If you say so." I pulled a USB key out of my pocket and held it up. "Who wants this?"

Will Hale took the key from me, plugged it into a slot, and started clicking the mouse on the computer.

"This better be good," Stone warned me. "We don't take on a lot of people. You're here because Juliet tolerates you, Finn Wiley likes you, and Sienna vouches for you. That's it."

I forgot how nervous I was and turned my attention to Stone. I gave him a shit-stirring grin that said, *Your girlfriend liked me before she met you, and you know it.* He narrowed his eyes. Then Will clicked a button, and my music came over the speakers.

I'd recorded four songs. I wrote the first one slowly, but surprisingly, the other three came fast, within a few hours' time. I'd put the equipment Finn gave me to good use. I'd recorded the guitar parts and the vocals using the microphone, and then I'd composed electronic bass, drums, and key parts and layered them in. Electronic sounds were never as good as live instruments, and a real album would have all live musicians. But for a demo I made by myself with no studio and no instruments besides a guitar, it was the best I would get.

Less than a minute into the first song, my brain unscrambled itself and I remembered: this music was good. I'd made it because I liked it.

It sounded nothing like Seven Dog Down. The music I'd written borrowed heavily from blues, mixed with a catchy riff and a funky beat. It matched well with my singing voice, which had always had a natural smoky roughness to it. I drew out that roughness in the demo vocals, emphasizing it, drawling out some of the words. It was music for a wicked party, music that made you want to bop in your chair, music for spying someone sexy across the room and making a move, music for singing along in your car with your buddy or your girl. It wasn't music that changed your life, but it was music that reminded you that life was, in fact, a lot of fun sometimes if you let go.

As we spun into the third song, I leaned back in my chair. I tugged my hood off and linked my fingers behind my neck, stretching out my elbows.

When the fourth song finished and silence fell, I looked around the room at the Road Kings. "Admit it," I said. "You liked it. I'm a genius."

Will cleared his throat. I pointed at him. "Your boy here likes it. He just doesn't want to say."

"I like it," Will admitted. "The genius comment is a bit much, but I like the music."

I turned in my chair to look at Sienna, who was standing back, leaning against the wall. She gave me a wide-eyed, excited look and a thumbs up. I winked at her.

"Sienna likes it," I told the room, turning back around.

"Okay, okay," Neal Watts said. "Knock it off. It's good." He looked at the other band members. "You know it is."

"It's passable," Stone said, still giving me a glare. It seemed to be his usual expression.

"The drums in the second song," Axel said. "I know exactly what I would do. A real drummer, a good one, would send it to the next level."

"I know," I agreed. "I tried it a lot of different ways, and I couldn't quite get it right. I ran out of time."

"Denver?" Neal said, and the room went quiet, waiting for their lead singer's opinion.

Denver scratched his chin, thinking. His dark hair was grown into messy curls, though his beard was neatly trimmed. He had gray eyes and dark lashes. Some women thought Denver was even better looking than me, but they were wrong. Being better looking than me wasn't possible.

"How much do I hate that it's actually good?" Denver finally asked the room. "A lot. I hate it a lot."

I pumped my fist, and the first thought I had was, *I can't wait to tell Katie about this.* She was going to be so excited. "I *am* a genius," I said.

"You're not," Denver replied calmly. "You really are not. But I know good music when I hear it, man, and that's good stuff. You have a full album of that?"

"No sweat," I said, even though there *would* be sweat to come up with ten more songs. A lot of sweat. Maybe another couch crying session. Or two.

"Then I owe Finn Wiley fifty bucks," Denver said. "He bet me that you'd come up with something good that we'd actually want to record, and I didn't believe him."

I gave Denver my most winning smile. "Never bet against me, man," I told him. "I hope you learned your lesson."

NINETEEN

Katie

"WILLAMETTE PARK," Gwen said.

"Guilty," I said to the phone I'd propped on the bed while I sorted my clothes.

"Outside Hollywood Vintage clothing store. In the bar of the Sapphire Hotel."

"Guilty of both." I smiled as I took a shirt from a hanger.

"I know you're guilty," Gwen said. She was in her L.A. apartment, scrolling on her phone as she talked to me on her iPad. "I've seen it. I never thought I would say this, but do you have to kiss your boyfriend quite so much?"

I rummaged through my underwear, still smiling. In the two weeks since I'd first slept with Travis, we'd done a good amount of kissing in public. When your public kisses are photographed and posted to social media, it might seem like too much.

It wasn't too much. At all.

"It's impulsive," I explained to my assistant. "He's my boyfriend. People kiss their boyfriends—it isn't news. No one has to look, and they definitely don't have to take pictures."

"I can sort of understand it," Gwen said, still scrolling. "He's hot, but you don't have to—Wait, you kissed him in Powell's Books?"

"I couldn't help it." I grabbed another hanger. "We were book shopping together, Gwen. *Book shopping.* And he was standing in the aisle, holding books that *he actually reads*, and he looked so cute, and I just walked up and kissed him."

"Okay, that one, I understand," she admitted. "Any man looks hot while book shopping, but Travis White is next level. I can't decide whether this picture is sexy or annoying."

"It's sexy," I supplied. It had been a great kiss—spontaneous, enthusiastic, sweet. I'd melted into Travis without thinking. It went without saying that we'd forgotten our original rule to discuss kissing before it happened. Now we just did it whenever we wanted.

"Katie, PDA is so out of style," Gwen argued. "It's uncool. No one does this sappy stuff anymore."

"I'll tell you what. When you're dating the hottest guy you've ever seen, then you don't have to kiss him in public. Or ever. I don't care. But he's my boyfriend, and if I want to kiss him in a bookstore, then I will."

A throat cleared softly behind me, and I turned to see Travis standing at the top of the loft stairs, leaning on one hip, listening to me. He looked pleased.

Gwen couldn't see him on her screen, so she kept talking. "Okay, you're in your Hot Girl era. I get it. The comments are mostly positive." She scrolled, scanning Instagram comments, which she spent more time doing these days so that I wouldn't have to. "People think you're cute. They like the clothes I got you. They think Travis looks fuckable. There are rumors of a new album. The negatives—except for the usual unhinged assholes—are that Travis is going to break your heart because he's an unreliable jerk. Also, *you're* going to break *his* heart, because you're using him for sex while he's actually in love. Basically, you two are doomed."

I glanced at Travis. His smile had dimmed, and he looked thoughtful. "Anything else I need to know?" I asked Gwen.

"Not really, just people with no lives commenting online. Between us, though, you look better than you did when you left L.A. You said you were orgasmed out, and I didn't believe you, but now I think he must have upped his game, because lately you really *are* orgasmed out—"

"Bye, Gwen." I jabbed the screen to end the call. I turned to Travis—to apologize, maybe—but he had moved closer and was already behind me. Without speaking, he put his hands on my shoulders, squeezing gently, then rubbing.

My mind went blank with pleasure. I leaned back into the firm warmth of his chest and closed my eyes. His fingers massaged expertly up the sides of my neck, his thumbs working the back of my neck under my hair. He smelled good.

"Sorry about Gwen," I managed to say, trying to sound rational through the waves of heat that were spiraling through my body.

Travis's response was a noncommittal *mmm* sound. His hands continued their magic. I felt his calluses from guitar playing against my skin, and it turned me on even more.

I leaned my weight back into him, letting my muscles relax into jelly. He was lean and warm, familiar. My blood flushed hot. His hands left my neck and dropped to my waist, where he lifted the hem of my shirt just enough to sneak under it. His palms caressed my belly, then up, where they cupped my breasts over my bra. He lowered his mouth to the side of my neck and kissed me there. I let out a gasp of pleasure that was mixed with an embarrassing groan.

"We keep doing this," I managed to say.

"Yeah," he replied.

We hadn't stopped after that first night. We probably should have, but then there was the next night, and the night after that. There was morning sex with Travis, and making out with Travis on the sofa while we tried to watch TV, which led to even more sex with Travis. Every time, my brain repeated, *Just one more time. Why not? What could it hurt? Just this once. And then again. Just this once.*

Just this once, I thought as his fingers drew down the cups of my bra and brushed over my nipples.

For the last two weeks, I hadn't had to think about how to play a sex goddess who was having a wild fling with a rock star. Because I was one.

"We have to," Travis reasoned, his voice hoarse against my skin. "You're leaving." To say he had been enthusiastic over the last two weeks was an understatement. He was as horny as I was. He was skilled. He was attentive. He could go fast or slow with equal creativity. He seemed to have made a map of my body and memorized it, because he knew everything.

"I have to go back to L.A.," I said reluctantly. "You know that. It's only for a few days." He had to stay in Portland to finish some of the work on his new album, but he was going to follow me to L.A. when he was finished.

"The premiere of *The Love Fix-Up*," he promised, the words warm against my skin. *The Love Fix-Up* was the movie I'd shot before *High School Reunion*, and it was about to release. "I'll be there."

"It won't be a big deal," I said for the dozenth time. Netflix premieres were industry events, not spectacles. There would be some press there and a few photographers, as well as the cast, the producers, the director. We'd take photos outside the theater, then watch the movie inside. The cast would appear onstage afterward and answer questions for twenty minutes. Then there would be the inevitable party, and we'd all go home. It would not be an earth-moving news story.

But it was going to be our first official public appearance as a couple. Travis had told me about how my name had softened the Road Kings' reception of him, and Stella had sent me another script that was offered to me because I'd accepted the thriller script, and word was getting out that I wasn't typecast in romcoms anymore. The message she sent with the script was simply: *It's working.*

I didn't care about that as Travis's hands moved to my back and unclasped my bra. We were going to be apart for four whole days until he joined me in L.A. The thought made my body ache. I turned around in his arms, put my arms around his neck, and kissed him.

We did a *lot* of kissing—Gwen was right about that. What we did in public were quick kisses, affectionate and sweet, and they were nothing compared to what we did when we were alone. We made out as much as we had sex. In the kitchen while making dinner. In the shower. In bed, long sessions that turned into agonizing foreplay, his mouth and hands moving slowly down my body until I lost my mind. Kissing me—all over —seemed to be Travis's new hobby.

I'd often thought I needed a new hobby in my life, something outside of my job. Marathon running? Art collecting? As I lifted my arms for Travis to pull my shirt and bra off, I thought, *Looks like I found my hobby.*

Just this once, I added. *Because I'm leaving. What could it hurt? Just this once.*

I shoved my clothes aside on the bed as Travis lowered me onto my back. His expert tongue circled my nipple, and as I spiraled toward bliss, he lifted his mouth and said, "I read your script."

My wobbly brain took a moment to process what he was talking about. What script? Wait—he didn't mean—

I dug my hands into his hair in a way that was unmistakable, and he stopped what he was doing. "You read my script?"

Travis looked up at me from between my bare breasts, this decadent man that I got to indulge in like dessert every day. His blue gaze was hazy. "You left it open on your laptop while you were in the shower," he explained. "I read it. It's good."

"It's nothing," I said, trying not to panic. No one knew I was writing a script—not Stella, not Gwen, no one. "It's a side thing I work on every once in a while when I have time. It isn't finished."

"It's funny," Travis said.

"It isn't a thing," I insisted. "It won't get made or anything. It's just an idea I had, and I played around with whether it would work, and I never finished it, and—it's nothing."

It seemed to occur to him slowly that I might be panicking a bit. "All right," he said.

"Because I'm not a writer."

He nodded slowly, but said, "You wrote something, though. I think that makes—"

"No. I didn't finish it. I'm not a screenwriter." The idea was absurd. I was an actor—show up, say lines, go home. Actors and screenwriters were different species, oil and water in Hollywood. Writers thought actors were good-looking dummies. Actors thought writers were deeply weird nerds. End of story.

And yet I gripped Travis's hair tighter. "You thought it was good?"

The thoughts cleared behind his eyes and he smiled lazily. "Yeah, I did."

"You thought it was funny?" I asked, because I was pathetic.

"It is."

"What part specifically? What did you laugh at?"

His grin expanded. Ignoring my grip on his hair, he pressed up and kissed the corner of my mouth, his touch soft. "I'll tell you later," he said. "I was about to give you your going-away present."

I made a sound of frustration. He pulled away from me, leaned back, and pulled his shirt off, tossing it. My gaze moved hypnotized over his tawny skin, his dark flat nipples, his collarbones. Those tattoos. While I watched, he placed a hand on his bare chest, then slid it slowly down over his flat stomach toward his happy trail and the button of his pants. His eyes were alight with suppressed laughter. The man knew exactly what he was doing.

"Tell me," I insisted.

Travis sighed. His hand stopped tantalizingly on the skin below his belly button, his fingertips notched behind the waist of his jeans. He looked at the ceiling as if recalling with difficulty.

"It's all funny," he said, "but I laughed out loud at the dinner scene."

I forgot that I was topless as I felt a warm glow at those words. "You did?"

Travis nodded. "The banter is great in that scene. I also loved the soccer game. You have your characters come together in that one, and it's funny, but it also really works."

I stared up at him, amazed. My unfinished script was called *Loser Academy*. It was about a teenage girl who gets sent to a boarding school for losers, where—if I ever finished the script—she would become the school's unlikely leader and hero.

No one else had ever read it until now—until Travis. And

Travis thought it was funny. Not just that, he thought it was good.

I blinked up at him. He was so beautiful to me in that moment, it was like staring at the sun.

He looked down at me, oblivious. "You should finish the script, Katie," he said. "There, I said it. Can I go back to what I was doing?"

"I want to have sex with you so much right now," I said back. "You have no idea."

His features softened in surprise, and then he laughed. He leaned down, bracing himself above me, and took my bottom lip between his teeth, making me shiver before he let it go. Then he kissed me properly, deep and expert, his mouth exploring mine slowly at first, then more urgently.

There was something wrong with having this much pleasure, I thought as he kissed down to my breasts again. There had to be a catch. Our relationship was fake—was that the catch? The thought touched down and then flitted away again, weightless. The word *fake* meant nothing when Travis's fingers hooked into the waistband of my leggings and my underwear, tugging them down as he kissed my belly. When he pulled everything off as he went to his knees on the floor next to the bed.

"I'm going to kiss you at the airport," he said, teasing me. "But first, I'm going to kiss you the way I like to."

I blacked out after that. He loved doing this, and he was so, so good at it. I would never get used to the things he made me feel, sensations I didn't have names for and couldn't explain. I wasn't used to the pleasure he took in it, as if my enjoyment fed his and made it stronger. I wasn't used to how fast he could make me come, when usually it took forever and had to follow a specific set of criteria. I kept thinking the last time must have been chance, that it wouldn't happen that way again. And then it did.

Just this once. One more time, just to see if it happens. One more.

When I had finished, he rose up and rolled on a condom. He bent my knees and pressed them to my chest, and when he came into me it changed the sensation so much that I orgasmed all over again. When Travis finished, too, I looked at the sheen of sweat on his skin and thought that four days apart would feel like forever.

WHEN WE HAD DRESSED, we lay on the bed, talking softly, reluctant to move. I really should pack my suitcase and get ready, but I wanted to put it off for a few more minutes.

I was snuggled into the crook of his neck, feeling his body radiate heat through his T-shirt, when he picked up his phone from the nightstand. He angled it above us and took a photo of us, a closeup of our faces relaxed together on the pillow.

"What are you doing?" I asked, though I already knew.

"You said we're not official until it's on Instagram," he said. "Fuck it. I think we're official."

I smiled as he tapped on the photo. It was a great photo. We looked good. We looked happy.

Travis paused, waiting for me to object. There was supposed to be a schedule, I remembered. I should consult with Stella about when the right time was.

"Do it," I said. "Fuck it."

I felt his body vibrate with a quiet chuckle. "I'm a bad influence on you."

"That's the idea."

He tapped open Instagram, bypassing thousands of notifications he hadn't read, and started a new post. "Last chance."

"Do it," I said again.

As I watched, he uploaded the photo and typed the caption: *The best way to spend time with my girl. XO.* He hit Post, then exited Instagram and tossed his phone back on the nightstand.

He'd just announced to millions of fans that I was his girlfriend.

Things were about to get real.

TWENTY

Travis

BEING BACK in L.A. wasn't as bad as I thought it would be. Sure, it was smoggy and dry. The memories were bad. I was still homeless. But I had half of a new record finished back in Portland, and my girlfriend was here. Even I could see that things were looking up.

My Uber dropped me at the gates at the foot of Andy's driveway. I buzzed his security system and waved at the camera above my head. The gates swung open with a click.

I walked up the driveway with my duffel bag slung over my shoulder like a hobo in an old movie. Andy's front door opened and he stood on the step, hands on his hips, wearing a faded Hawaiian shirt and cutoff jean shorts that were cut too high on the thigh for everyone else's comfort except his.

"You're like the clap," he said when I reached the steps. "I can't get rid of you."

"I missed you, you old crustacean," I said. I dropped my bag at my feet and hugged him.

"Oof," he said as he slapped his palms on my back. "I see you've been reading your dictionary." When I let him go, he gave me a scowl. "Care to explain why my second ex-wife is here?"

I grinned at him. Andy's second—and final—wife, Elena, had been one of Hollywood's top stylists in the nineties. She was tall, flawless, and of foggy Eastern European heritage. Even though she and Andy had divorced a decade ago, she still came by to hook up with him on a regular basis—something I knew because I had encountered her on many a morning after, walking in a dignified manner down the stairs and through the kitchen while I ate my breakfast or while I lounged by the pool. I had realized early that lecturing Andy on the inadvisability of ex sex was a bad idea. At over sixty, Andy knew what he was doing, and so did Elena. If they wanted some no-strings nookie, it was nothing to do with me.

But I figured that I had met Elena on enough walks of shame to call her up and ask for wardrobe advice. She had agreed, and here we were, meeting at Andy's house.

"Admit it," I said to Andy. "You're happy she had an excuse to come over. How long since you banged her?"

He glanced at his tanned wrist, where he had never worn a watch in his life. "Forty minutes or so. Maybe forty-five."

"You're welcome," I said, brushing past him into the house. "Now she and I can get down to business."

Elena was in the living room, where she had wheeled in a clothing rack. She slid hangers down the rack, rearranging garment bags. Her salt-and-pepper hair was tied up in a complicated twist, and she wore fashionable black-framed glasses, a dramatic one-shoulder top, and jeans that fit her like a second skin. The work she'd had done on her face—and her boobs at some point—was top shelf. It wasn't a mystery to me why Andy still slept with her. She was out of my age range, but she was a straight-up babe.

I smiled a greeting at her and stepped forward to take her hand, but she gave me a frosty look over the top of her glasses frames. "You," she said to me in her Eastern European accent. "You look terrible. For a pretty man, you dress ugly."

I plucked her hand from her waist and held it in both of mine. "I need your help, Your Majesty." I pressed a kiss to the back of her hand. "I, a lowly peasant in the world of fashion, beg for your royal assistance."

She made a face. "Ugh. What is this?" She waved up and down in front of me, indicating my jeans and leather jacket. "You have no clothes. I know because I have seen you naked next to the pool. I said to Andy, Why do you have a naked boy by your pool? He said, Naked boy is sad, leave him be. Now you want to stop being naked. So I brought you clothes."

I shifted my weight. I hadn't thought I was naked quite so much during my low period. "Uh, sorry about that. I was going through something, you know, I was kind of—"

"I do not care," Elena declared. "Your sadness does not concern me. Your clothes concern me. I have dressed many beautiful men. Brad Pitt. Luke Perry. Jon Bon Jovi would not hire me, and look how *he* dresses." She shook her head. "I knew the waist size of Bruce Willis. Robert Downey Jr. called me for every event, until—" She broke off and looked away.

"Elena is sensitive about Robert Downey Jr.," Andy said softly next to me.

"I don't wish to speak of him," Elena said, making me feel like she was chiding me, even though she had brought him up.

"Sure," I said. I motioned to the clothing rack. "You didn't have to go to this trouble, Elena. I only wanted you to give me some pointers."

"I do not give *pointers*," she declared. "I dress people. I dress men. It's my calling."

I glanced at Andy. He smiled at me.

Elena had retired from styling, but I hadn't known until this moment that she hadn't wanted to quit. I could suddenly see what had happened: from being sought after in the nineties, the bookings and phone calls had started drying up, and there had been less and less demand. She had faded out of the business—Hollywood was ruthless with women over forty—but she missed it. Elena was pretending to do me a favor, but without thinking, I had actually done one for her.

I pointed at the garment bags on the rack. "These are for me?"

"I made some calls," Elena said. "I know exactly what you should wear to a premiere. This is child's play for me."

"You don't know my measurements."

She gave me her frosty look. "If I see a man naked, I know his measurements. So I know yours."

"Right. We should stop bringing that up, maybe."

Andy laughed.

I looked at him. "Why didn't you tell me to wear clothes?"

"I did," he said. "Plenty of times."

I sighed. "Okay, we're moving on. Let's see."

I had a moment of doubt before Elena unzipped the first garment bag. She was good at her job, but she hadn't dressed anyone in a while. What if the clothes she picked belonged in 2005?

Then she showed me the first outfit. And the second.

Andy whistled. "Nice."

Elena unzipped the third garment bag.

I looked at her. "You know I don't have any money, right? These look expensive."

Elena snapped her fingers. "I make some calls, the

designers give me clothes. I told them your name. You're a singer like Andy. Your girlfriend is a beautiful actress. Everyone loves her, loves both of you. You are very popular on the TikTok. The designers want you to wear their clothes so they can see them on the TikTok. They gave me the clothes I choose for free."

She unzipped more bags, then opened boxes. Tuxes for the premiere, casual clothes, jackets. Shoes. Accessories. Watches. Jewelry.

A whole new wardrobe worth six figures, delivered in a few days. Because I was popular on the TikTok. Because of Katie.

I was famous again. Because of Katie.

Our fake relationship was working.

I missed her like crazy. The last time I'd seen her was at PDX, where I'd kissed her in front of the crowd, just like we planned. After I'd kissed her everywhere else in our bedroom.

I didn't like this. It felt fucking weird. Did Katie think that I was dating her just to get free clothes? That I was sleeping with her for the same reason? Did she think I was doing all of it just because I was broke?

The comments her assistant read to her over the phone came back to me. According to the internet, I looked fuckable, but either I was going to screw Katie over, or she was going to break my heart. There was no third option.

But there was no way out now. I was here for the premiere. Katie wanted her role with Edgar Pinsent, and she deserved it. That was what this was about. Turning down these clothes—aside from the fact that it would hurt Elena's feelings, which would make Andy mad—would be stupid and unproductive. I needed good clothes. The premiere was what Katie wanted, so it was what I would do.

I stepped forward and kissed Elena on the cheek. "You absolute goddess," I declared. "I love all of it. Thank you."

She held up a hand, but I knew she was pleased. "It was no trouble." She turned to Andy. "He isn't so bad. Tell him to try it all on."

"Marry me again," Andy said to her, and I thought he meant it.

"Stop asking me," Elena said. "It is physical only. We agreed."

He sighed.

I picked up one of the tuxes from the rack. I would change upstairs, because from this day forward, neither of these two would see me naked ever again. "You should marry him again, Elena," I advised her. "I would."

"No," she said to me. "Once was enough. Now go put clothes on."

I did.

TWENTY-ONE

Katie

HAD I said that the premiere wasn't a big deal? That it wouldn't be news? This premiere, apparently, was news.

I didn't notice at first. While we were being driven to the theater in our hired car, I was distracted by staring at my maybe-fake boyfriend, who looked so good it made my eyes hurt. He was stretched out in the seat next to me, looking back at me.

I hadn't seen Travis after I left Portland until twenty minutes ago, when my car had picked him up from the gates of Andy Rockweller's house. I'd left a scruffy musician in Portland, but now he was clean shaven, his hair freshly cut and styled. And the suit—the suit looked like it had been made for him. Black, molded to his long legs and his lean hips and shoulders, the lapels dark blue satin that gave off a classy sheen. Contrasting the darkness was the shirt underneath—brilliant turquoise blue, a shade that matched his eyes. I had seen this man in rock star leather jackets, in sweatpants, in nothing at all. I had never seen him like this.

"You said you didn't have any good clothes," I said, as starstruck as if I was a groupie meeting him backstage at a concert.

Travis shrugged, his gaze never leaving me. "I called in a favor with a stylist I know."

"And he found this suit for you?"

"She did, yes." When he saw my expression, he laughed softly. "Relax, Katie. She's Andy's ex-wife."

"Elena Petrova?" I gasped.

"You know her?"

"I know who she is. Of course I do. She was a big deal a few decades ago, and no one talks about her anymore, but I remember. You're saying Elena Petrova came out of retirement to dress you?"

"It was a favor," Travis said again. His gaze moved down my dress, then back up, taking its time lingering over my cleavage, then to my face. "You look beautiful," he said.

He said that often, and he'd already said it when he first got in the car, but I felt a blush all over again. I really did like this dress. It was dark red and cut low enough in the front to be daring. I'd added red lipstick, which I never wore. "Gwen found the dress," I said.

"She has good taste." He picked up my hand and squeezed it in his, making me feel warm all over. Then he said, "What's the plan for tonight?"

"Plan?" I asked.

"Do you want me to do anything specific? I feel like a kiss would be a bit much at an event like this. We don't want to overdo it."

My pulse clanged in my ears. The script. He was talking about the script. We were official now, ever since his Instagram post, and we were supposed to act like it. "I don't have any specific plans," I managed to say. "You're right that, er, kissing would be too much. But we'll need to look affectionate."

"I can do that," Travis said.

"There will be red carpet interviews," I went on. "They might ask how we met."

"The Lakers game." He nodded. "Got it."

Right. We'd met at the Lakers game, not in Andy's kitchen, where I'd propositioned him with our deal. Where he'd read the script I'd written and printed out for him. That script had said *premiere or awards show optional*.

He was still holding my hand in his. I hadn't seen him in four days. He'd kissed me at the airport with his hands cradling my face, slow and romantic. Pictures of it had made Instagram. Did he think that was all I wanted from him? To have a date to a premiere and make Instagram?

He was staying at Andy's while he was in L.A. We hadn't discussed him staying with me in my apartment. He hadn't come because I hadn't invited him. I opened my mouth to ask if he'd pack his bag tonight and stay with me instead, but then I heard the noise.

I turned to the window. We were pulling up in front of the theater. "What is that sound?" I asked.

Travis leaned past me to look out the window, and he smiled. "Fans."

They were already cheering as our car pulled up, as if they knew who was in it. When Travis opened his door and stood, it became a roar. I sat stunned as Travis circled to my door, opened it, and took my hand to help me out. I nearly choked when I saw what was happening.

At a normal premiere, we'd get maybe a dozen autograph seekers. This was L.A., where a premiere of a third-rate Netflix movie was hardly an event. The people here saw celebrities more famous than me at Trader Joe's every day.

The scene tonight was chaos. There were hundreds of fans lining the street, jostling along the red carpet security line, bumping into photographers and industry executives. Some of them held up signs. TRAVIS WE LOVE YOU. MARRY ME TRAVIS. And one waved by a teenaged girl, the sign spangled with glitter and hearts: TRAVIS+KATIE.

The sight of Travis drove them wild. They waved and screamed, making the unprepared and underpaid theater security guards wave them back from the car. The photographers given this boring assignment had turned away from the red carpet, and all of them were shooting Travis and me instead. They looked surprised and excited. The security guards looked worried. Our driver looked confused, because the crowd had moved in front of our car, and now he couldn't drive away to park.

But Travis...Travis bloomed. His posture straightened and his expression lit up at the crowd, the noise, the chaos. Holding my hand in his, he turned to me, his blue eyes sparkling. "Go with it," he said.

I didn't have the chance to ask what he meant. He tugged me toward the crowd and raised a hand in a wave, greeting them all. They responded, chanting and screaming his name.

This wasn't a premiere, this was a rock concert. I'd expected a dull industry event like dozens I'd been to before, but instead I was tugged into a crowd of adoring fans—right *into* the crowd. Because instead of standing politely back and waving at the people who had come to see him, Travis stepped past a security guard, unhooked the rope barrier from its post, and walked into the thick of the people, still holding my hand.

I didn't have time to panic, and I didn't need to. People greeted us, cheered, took photos and selfies. People put pens in our hands and asked us to sign things. I signed a woman's white T-shirt and a young man's arm. Fans hugged Travis, hooked their arms around his shoulders and took selfies with him. He tugged me toward him, put his arm around my waist, and people took pictures of both of us. Travis waved over the girl with the TRAVIS+KATIE sign, and we both autographed it for her.

We made our way through the thick of the crowd to the far edge, where a security guard was gesturing us toward the red carpet. "Okay, we gotta go," I heard Travis say to the fans. "We have to do this premiere. Thank you! I love you!" Another wild cheer went up. I gripped his hand and found myself on the red carpet as the security guard waved the crowd back behind us.

People were staring at us. Photographers were still taking pictures and videos. Travis ignored it all and turned to me. "You all right?" he asked.

I nodded. I was flustered, but that had been fun. I could see why people got addicted to the rock star life. "Do I look okay?" I asked. Travis's collar was askew, so I reached up and adjusted it back to perfection.

"You're gorgeous," Travis said, brushing a hand down the back of my dress and aligning the seam. He tucked back a loose lock of my hair and grinned at me. "Let's do this."

"People are mad," I whispered, leaning in. "We've messed up the order of things."

"They'll get over it," he said. "Your turn. You lead, I'll follow."

I led him down the red carpet. Travis was a pro—he knew exactly where to stand, what to do. He stood by my shoulder, letting me have the spotlight but never getting too far away. His hand always rested lightly on my lower back, my middle back, or in mine. He answered questions without hogging attention. He had done a million publicity events, and it showed. He hit every mark, followed every cue. He was nothing like the man who had spent months next to Andy Rockweller's pool, too lost and depressed to put clothes on.

I relied on my own years of practice as the red-carpet questions came fast and furious.

"Katie, has Travis seen this movie? Has he seen any of your movies?"

"How did you two meet?"

"Is Travis going to do a cameo in one of your films?"

"That was quite a reception you two got. How does it feel to date a rock star?"

"Will you go on his next tour with him?"

When we got inside the theater, it got weirder, because those were the Hollywood people. Men I had never met before introduced themselves to me—every executive, writer, and producer who had come tonight. *The Love Fix-Up*'s director, who had been so checked out that he called me Cathy at least three times during filming, was suddenly my best friend, pumping my hand in a shake and telling me how happy he was to see me. A terrifying woman who was a high-level Netflix executive kissed me on both cheeks and said we "should have a meeting." I didn't know what that meant. No one at Netflix had ever asked me for a meeting.

My co-star, Jason, swept in to pose for photos with me with a grin, his veneers glowing. He, too, was suddenly nicer to me than he'd ever been while we were shooting. "Katie," someone called as we posed, "will Travis have a problem watching you two kissing in the movie?"

"I don't think so," I said.

From the sidelines, Travis called out, "I'm a very confident guy." Everyone laughed.

It was perfect. Travis was perfect, and so was I. It was exactly what I'd planned with this fake relationship.

I held his hand as we took our seats in the theater and the lights went down. I didn't know how hard I was squeezing it until Travis leaned over in the dark and whispered in my ear, "Is everything all right? Did I do something wrong?"

I loosened my grip on his hand and shook my head. "No," I whispered back. "You're amazing."

"I'm not actually going to enjoy watching you kissing that guy," he said, and I smiled. The panic in my chest loosened. Why was I panicking? I couldn't think of a reason.

I was going to tell Travis that Jason wasn't nearly as good a kisser as he was—no one came close—but before I could speak, Travis leaned over and whispered again. "Do you want to ditch the afterparty? I know an amazing late-night teppanyaki bar."

I felt the tension flow out of my shoulders. I could breathe again. I didn't want to be on display anymore, following the script. I just wanted him.

"Yeah," I whispered back, squeezing his hand. "I do."

TWENTY-TWO

Travis

SUDDENLY, everything moved fast.

After eighteen months of no schedule, no career, and no love life, I could barely keep up. Days flew by, then weeks, then months, with hardly a moment to breathe.

I spent most of my time in Portland, working on the new album. I recruited a band, wrote songs, and recorded in the Road Kings' studio, usually in sessions that lasted fourteen hours or more. Finn produced the album, and we spent days rewriting, rerecording, and remixing, often with Finn playing instruments himself. Finn could play anything.

Katie was in L.A.—except when she was in New York for meetings or in Portland visiting me. She'd had an explosion of offers recently, and she went into prep and rehearsals for *Honor Student*. She was nervous about her first thriller, and whenever we were together, we ran lines, with me reading all of the other roles so she could practice. It didn't matter that I was the worst actor in history. We still had fun.

I traveled to L.A. to do publicity and interviews to get people excited about the new album. We had started to plan a tour—my first ever solo tour—and the dates and cities were being worked out. I needed a road crew, a set list, rehearsals. There was a publicity tour planned for when the album released.

The Love Fix-Up was the most successful movie Katie had ever released, probably because it came out after she was dating me. I had stopped being rat poison in the music business again, probably because I was dating Katie. I hated two things about this setup: one, that I no longer gave a shit about what Katie could do for my career, and two, that I didn't see her nearly enough.

When Katie went to Austin to shoot on location for *Honor Student*, I took a break from recording and flew in to join her. Even then, we didn't have enough time, because she was on set for ten hours a day. I visited the set, took pictures with the cast and crew, made nice with everyone, and fooled around with my girlfriend in her trailer between takes. I also tired her out in her hotel room every night until she fell asleep. She had to work off her anxiety somehow, and I was happy to help.

But then I had to go back to Portland, and Katie had to go back to L.A. before she could take any time to come stay with me—and we went in a circle again.

The internet was fascinated with us. The KatieWatch account had passed three hundred thousand followers, a fact I forcibly blocked from my mind. There were a dozen videos on it from the premiere, including one of Katie straightening my collar on the red carpet while I adjusted her dress. It had over eight million views. Even Jonathan had started giving me social media updates. *Your Instagram has four million followers. Don't you think you should post something?* By *something*, he meant another selfie of Katie and me. I hadn't posted one after the picture of us in bed. The only post I'd put up in the last few months was a selfie of me at the Road Kings' studio, with the caption *New album coming by the end of the year, I promise. See you soon on the road.*

I didn't want to post another picture of Katie and me. The more famous we both got, the less comfortable I felt. This wasn't an arrangement to me anymore—even though it was, and we were both benefiting.

If I ever wanted Katie to take me seriously as a boyfriend—for real—I needed my career back. Katie didn't need a man who sat depressed and naked by his friend's pool or who cried on the sofa in his other friend's borrowed apartment. She deserved better. I needed to be better than that. So I needed the fake relationship in order to be good enough for a real one. How's that for a mindfuck?

Edgar Pinsent delayed the start of his next film for a month, and then another. I could do this. By the time Katie didn't need me anymore and our deal was over, I'd convince her that I was a man she'd want to be with in real life. If I had enough time, I could make it happen.

After my final day of recording the album—which I had titled *The Lowest Equation*—I called Katie. It was July, and Portland was ridiculously beautiful. I hadn't seen much of the summer while I was holed up inside RKS. I watched the sun set out the window of the loft as I sat on the sofa, wishing that I wasn't here alone.

"Hi," Katie said when she answered the phone. She sounded pleased and tired at the same time.

"Hey," I said. "Where are you? Are you busy?"

"I just got back to my apartment. Did you finish the record?" She knew this was my last day in the studio.

"I did," I said.

She gave a squeal of excitement. "Yes! When do I get to hear it?"

I'd been putting off letting Katie hear the songs I'd written, but she wouldn't let me do it any longer. "I'll send it to you after we hang up. You can listen to it tonight."

"At last."

"I wanted to get it right before you heard it. It needed to be perfect."

"I'm sure it's perfect, Travis. I can't wait."

I took a breath. "You have a break in your schedule, right?"

"I do. I have a week. There are just some meetings I need to—"

"Wait."

She went silent on the other end of the line. The word had come out sharper than I intended it to.

"I mean." I cleared my throat. "Um. Didn't the script you wrote for us have something in it about a vacation?"

There was a beat of silence, and I kicked myself for doing a normal phone call instead of FaceTiming her. I wished I could see her expression right now.

"The script had us going to Cabo," Katie said.

"Yeah, well, let's scrap that. They wouldn't leave us alone there, and I'm not keen on having pictures of my foxy girlfriend in a bikini all over the internet." I paused. "Unless you wanted to go."

"No," Katie said, and I *could* read her in that one word. She had been dreading the idea. "No bikini photos on the internet, please. I'd rather get bird flu."

"You don't need to get bird flu." I wiped beads of sweat from my forehead. *Be cool, man, be cool.* "How about visiting my parents instead?"

Shocked silence from Katie. "You want me to meet your parents?"

"I know it isn't in the script," I said quickly, "but they're good people. You'd like them. I haven't seen them in a long time. They're living in an RV, but my mom makes killer homemade no-bake granola bars, and my dad will probably give you a lesson on how to grow and harvest weed. They're in Washington right now, so we could drive, and since there's no room in the RV, we'd stay in a hotel. They'll love you." Why wasn't she saying anything? "It isn't a PR thing, but it's like method acting, you know? It'll keep us in character. Meeting my parents is something we'd do if we were really dating."

Her voice was impossible to read. "Travis, meeting the parents is something you do if the relationship is serious."

"We've been dating for three months," I said. "That's the story. People who are dating for three months can meet the parents. I think we should keep the story realistic." I squeezed my eyes shut, glad she couldn't see me. So much for being cool here. I was burying myself fast.

"You're serious?" she asked. "You really mean it?"

"Of course I do." Did she think I was fucking with her? I was dead serious when it came to Katie. "You don't have to decide now. You can think it over, or—"

"I'll do it," she said.

"Okay," I said, trying for cool again. "Okay, great. I'll arrange it."

"I have one condition."

"Anything."

"After we meet your parents, we go to Minnesota and meet mine."

A laugh bubbled out of me, pure relief. "Babe, I'd love to meet your parents."

"They're very square," she warned me, humor in her voice.

"Nice, but square. I guarantee they've never heard Seven Dog Down, and there's no weed in my dad's garden."

"I'll behave," I promised her. "Fly to Portland tomorrow, and we'll leave for my parents' tomorrow night."

After we hung up, I pulled up the final file of my new album on my phone. I composed a text to Katie and hovered my thumb over the Send button, trying not to panic.

It was stupid to be this anxious about her opinion. People had heard the album—everyone who worked on it, Finn, the Road Kings, Will Hale. Pretty soon, everyone in the world would be able to hear it if they wanted to. Why was I so terrified of Katie's opinion?

Because most of the songs were about her, that was why. Maybe she'd find that awkward. Maybe she wouldn't care. Maybe she wouldn't even notice.

It was too late to worry about it now. I tapped Send.

EVERY TIME I met Katie at the airport now, we got noticed. I usually had to sign autographs and take selfies with a few wrung-out travelers before Katie came out and we made our escape. I'd had to stop the show-off kisses because it started to feel weird to do it with everyone openly staring. I could have stopped meeting her at all, but that didn't feel right, either. Fake or real, she was my girlfriend, and I wanted to see her when she got off the plane to visit me.

More people noticed me today than the last time, which had been more than the time before. I had to contain my impatience and try not to be short with people as I took one selfie after another, but I kept the rock star charm turned on. "You're waiting for Katie?" one woman asked after she took a photo with me.

"I am," I said, smiling.

She smiled back. "When are you going to marry her? We're all waiting!"

Jesus. Was this what people talked about? I was saved from having to answer by the sight of Katie walking toward me, pulling her rolling suitcase while tugging her earbuds from her ears. "Excuse me," I said to the woman with—I hoped—believable politeness, and I jogged away.

People watched me approach Katie, watched me take her suitcase and put my arm around her shoulders. Katie snugged an arm around my waist—our usual pose, one we'd started doing because it looked good. We did it now because it was the quickest way through the crowd, which was pulling closer so people could see.

"We love you guys!" a girl's voice shouted.

"Get married!" someone else called—not the woman I'd been talking to, either. There were two people in this airport who thought it was cool to say that to a stranger.

Katie's arm flinched tighter around my waist, but she kept her gaze down as we walked through the doors and headed for my car. "Well, *that* made it weird," she said.

"Very weird," I agreed. "We need to rethink the airport pickups. I'll be spending more time in L.A. now that the album is finished."

Now that I was done recording, my homelessness was on my mind again. I wasn't going to sponge off of Finn for much longer. I had enough money to rent a place, but where? I liked Portland, and I still had work to do here. Los Angeles was where the heart of the music business was. It was also where Katie lived, and I wanted to be where she was. I made a mental note to ask Andy if he knew of anything good the next time I talked to him.

Katie was quiet as I put her suitcase into the back of my car.

I didn't like the serious look on her face. "What is it?" I asked as I shut the door. "What's wrong?"

She shook her head. "I can't put my finger on it." She looked beautiful, even after getting off an airplane, even in a jeans and tee with no makeup. I hadn't seen her in too long.

"Travis, the album—"

"You hate it," I said, half serious. "You can be honest. You think it sucks."

Her eyes widened. "What? No. Travis! I loved the album. I've been listening to it on repeat. It's incredible."

"You can admit you hate it," I said, stepping toward her. "It's a hack job, right?"

That got a smile out of her. She tapped her hand lightly against my stomach. "You're fishing for compliments."

"Me? Never." I kissed her then, because I couldn't not do it, because I couldn't be this close to her and not kiss her. I tilted her face up to mine and tasted her. Right in an airport parking garage that smelled like damp urine. What can I say? I'm a romantic guy.

When we broke apart, Katie said, "The album really is good."

"Okay," I said, looking into her eyes and trying to read what was wrong.

"I'm glad we're taking this vacation." She looked past me and around. "Something has changed. It's getting stressful. I can't explain it. I feel..." She trailed off.

"Yeah." I felt the same. I dropped a kiss to her forehead. "It'll be different in the wilds of Washington, I promise."

TWENTY-THREE

Travis

KATIE'S tense mood didn't lift. She was quiet on the drive back to the loft, and once we were inside, she turned and kissed me, tugging at my clothes.

We had done this a lot—every time we managed to occupy the same physical space while we worked in two different cities. It didn't matter that our relationship was fake, that no one saw this part of it, that this wouldn't get her a role with Edgar Pinsent or get me a record deal. We did it anyway. I couldn't think of a reason not to, and apparently, neither could she.

I hadn't had my hands on her in weeks. I kissed down the side of her neck the way she liked it, sucking gently on her skin —enough for her to feel it, not enough to leave marks. Katie gasped and unbuckled my belt, then opened the buttons on my jeans.

We were standing just inside the door—we'd barely made it

a few feet into the apartment. "We should slow down," I said, lifting my mouth from her skin.

Her reply was to slide her hand down into my jeans and cup me over my boxer briefs. Katie wasn't a Good Girl with me anymore. She knew me too well. She went after what she wanted, and she didn't apologize. I fucking loved it.

I pulled her T-shirt off over her head and threw it to the floor, leaving her in her bra. I pulled my shirt off, too, while her hand moved back to that amazing spot. I kissed her long and hard, then pulled away.

"Bedroom?" I asked.

Katie shook her head, her lips reddened and her skin flushed. "Too far."

"Yes, ma'am. The sofa it is."

We got there slowly, shedding clothes. It was the middle of a weekday, and either of us could have come up with a hundred things we should be doing, and yet there was nothing else but this, decadent and pleasurable. The world went by outside this apartment, but in here I would take the time to fuck my girlfriend until we were both spent. No questions. No demands. Just this.

I got Katie on her knees on the sofa, her hands braced on the arm. I knelt behind her and slid my hand down her belly, down where she wanted me to go. I took a moment to explore and figure out exactly what was going on down there. My body only had two modes—Off, which it had been in forever, and All the Way On. Katie's was more complicated. There was Hot Mode and Cool Mode—but there was also Cool But I Still Want To, Hot But it Takes a Minute, Hot But Not There, Hot But Sleepy, Cool But I Want To Make Out, Cool But Willing to Make You Happy, Hot But I Just Ate, Cool and Tipsy—the list went on. Plus there was a cycle in there, and her birth control pill, and—it was a lot. I had never studied anything in my life as hard as I studied Katie. I wanted to ace the test.

Today was definitely Hot Mode, mixed with Do It Quick and Don't Talk, and I was wildly happy to oblige. I kissed her neck and gently massaged one breast while I let my other hand do the talking. I got her close, then backed off, then did it again. She needed to get out of her head, needed to stop thinking and feel. I was good at that.

She finally unwound enough to come on my hand, letting it out with a long shudder. "Hands on the arm of the sofa," I said in her ear as she came down. "Brace yourself." As she did it, I dropped my hands to her hips.

We had done the health-check thing, followed by ditching condoms. We didn't talk about why we would do that for a relationship that was fake. I wasn't going to be the one to bring it up, because I just wanted more of her, everything I could get, for as long as she'd have me. I could convince her to be with me for real. I still had time.

It was dirty and fast and fantastic, urgent and sweet. When we were finished, I grabbed the blanket off the back of the sofa and wrapped it around us, lying down and pulling Katie close. She curled into me, snuggling as if she was worried I was going somewhere. I kissed her shoulder, and she sighed. We still had a five-hour drive tonight to the hotel I'd booked near my parents' campground in Washington, but it could wait. My girl needed a nap.

She hugged me tighter. Where did she think I was going?

It was the last thought I had before I dropped into sleep.

TWENTY-FOUR

Katie

BY SUNSET, we were past Seattle, Travis's Camaro growling hungrily over the interstate. My mood from the morning hadn't completely dissipated, but I felt better than I had. The panic had become faint background noise instead of a deafening roar.

I needed to talk about it, and with real life disappearing behind us, now was the time.

Travis had caught on that I was preoccupied. He'd done an incredible job pulling me out of it, because he was pure magic. The rest was up to me.

As he drove, I connected my phone to the car's sound system and played the song I'd listened to on repeat on the plane ride from L.A. It was from Travis's album, and it was called "Been There." The guitar was a catchy, snarly, low-key riff, the drums were irresistibly funky, and then Travis's unmistakable voice came in:

I'm livin' in nowhere
I told them I don't care
The one that gets me there
Is you

I watched Travis's brows rise in surprise as the song filled the car. Then he frowned, wondering what I was getting at. On the sound system, his voice growled the second verse:

I give 'em a wry grin
I tell you I'm tryin'
The way I'm surviving
Is you

My heart sped up and the panic came back. I had listened to the album over and over. It wasn't just good—it was really, *really* good. I wasn't a music critic, but the songs were catchy, melodic, cool. Travis's voice was a revelation, a sexy don't-give-a-fuck drawl. The lyrics were honest, self-deprecating, witty. Travis saw this album as a silly project no one would notice, a hail Mary for his career, but I didn't think so. I thought this album was going to be huge.

I sleep and I wake up
Beg you not to break up

I don't want to take up
Your time

You're my ambition
My luck and volition
It's just a condition
Of mine

I PAUSED THE SONG. "Travis, you *made* this? Like—you just *made* it?"

His gaze was on the road, his jaw tight. "What's wrong with it?"

"It's brilliant," I said. "I can't stop listening to it. Are the lyrics about me?"

It was an egotistical question. Maybe he was writing about some other woman he knew, one he wished he had back. Maybe he was writing about a fictional woman, and the songs were just a story.

But this song—and all of them, but particularly this one—made me want to cry, not because I didn't like the idea that he wrote about me, but because I did. I had never wanted anything as much as I wanted this song to be about me. If it wasn't about me, it would crush me.

If the song was part of our fake relationship—something he'd come up with to sell records—it would crush me.

Travis was quiet for a long moment, probably sensing that this question was a minefield in a way he hadn't figured out. "I wrote what I was thinking about at the time, so yeah, it's about you."

"It's about the real me? Or the fake me?"

He shook his head. "I don't understand. What are you getting at?"

"Are the songs about our fake relationship? Or our real one?"

"Katie." He ran his hand through his hair. "You're my only girlfriend. I was thinking about you when I wrote it. The real you. That's the only you I know."

He was as confused as I was, because the situation was confusing. We were supposed to be fake, but he'd written an album of songs about me, and I'd just spent an hour asleep against his naked body after incredible sex. Which meant we were real.

But he was about to become a superstar again, which meant publicity, tours, endless demands on him. Women and drugs thrown at him. He could be that guy again—the one he used to be. He'd have no room in his life for me anymore.

I told him the other thing I was thinking about, ever since I'd talked to Stella on the phone before getting on the plane in L.A.

"Edgar Pinsent is finished the script," I said. "He's leaving Romania and going into production. The money is lined up, and everything's a go."

Travis glanced at me, smiling, then turned back to the road. "That's great news. Right? It's what you've been waiting for."

I nodded, slumping back in my seat. "Stella has already talked to his assistant, and Edgar wants a meeting with me in London. I'm going after this vacation. If he casts me, I'm in, and the movie will shoot in Budapest. For three months."

"Okay." Travis nodded. "That's a long time, but we'll make it work. I'll come visit."

"You can't. Edgar's film shoots are notorious. He always shoots in obscure locations and makes the cast and crew stay away from all of their families and friends. He says that it immerses them more fully in the art and makes them give a more honest performance. It's how he gets so much intensity out of his actors onscreen."

"Oh." Travis blinked. "Well. I get that—I guess." He thought it over. "Three months is long, and it'll suck, being away from you. But it isn't forever. And it'll be worth it."

We drove in silence for a moment as the sky darkened into night. I was most likely going on a shoot for three months, and Travis would go on tour. It felt like we were two trains pulling out of a station in opposite directions. I looked out the window.

The phone call with Stella at the airport had put my mind in a spin. Before Travis, my life had had a comfortable routine—I did one romcom after another on a steady schedule, shooting mostly in L.A. The material was familiar, the schedule sane, and I knew I was good at my job. Now Stella was inundated with potential scripts, I had turned down all the romcoms on the table, I had just shot a thriller, and I was about to spend three months on location for the biggest job of my career. Stella and I talked almost every day.

"Listen," she'd said as I waited to board the plane, "I'm all for this vacation of yours, but check in with me daily, okay? We need to talk about the promo tour for *Honor Student*. I'm getting you on talk shows."

"Right," I'd said.

"We'll get that done before you disappear to Budapest. We'll also need to talk about the money you get offered from Edgar Pinsent when that comes through. I'll negotiate for as much as I can. Do you think the breakup with Travis should happen before Budapest or after?"

I'd wondered for a second if I had heard the words right. "What?"

"The breakup," she repeated, as if it was another item of business. "We should make a plan."

"Why?" I was already on edge, and the thought made my panic notch up higher. "We don't need to think about that yet. There's no rush."

"I didn't say there was a rush," Stella said calmly. "But you need to be strategic. You two are high profile, and the breakup will be news. I think we should maximize the benefits of the news breaking and use it to your advantage for extra publicity."

My stomach turned, and I thought I might be sick. The idea of getting through the craziest, most stressful time of my life without Travis was unthinkable. "Not yet," I said to Stella, keeping the desperation from my voice. "It isn't the right time yet."

"Maybe not, but it will be soon. Look, I know you like him, but Katie, please try to think logically here. You're about to star in an Edgar Pinsent film. It's going to win Oscars. If it's the right role, *you* could be nominated. This is it, honey—your shot at the best career you could possibly have. You have to take the shot from the best position, because you might not get another chance this good."

"I get that," I said as cold sweat broke out on my skin and my chest constricted. "I can do all of that with Travis. We don't need to break up."

"You're going on location, and he's going on tour," Stella pointed out. "He's a rock star, honey. What if he cheats on you? Being the pathetic one in a cheating scandal is *not* the look you want. It's best to protect yourself and get out before he has the chance to undo all of the good work you've done."

I could barely hear her past the blood pounding in my ears. "Travis wouldn't cheat on me."

Stella sighed. "A lot of rock stars' girlfriends have said those exact words. Just think about it. Look past how good-looking he is and make a plan. Are you looking to get married and have kids? Travis is just a stop on that road. Your relationship has worked perfectly. Now it's time to make a perfect exit before things get messy."

I looked over at Travis now, driving me to meet his parents. I had spent the plane ride after that phone call listening to the music this man had written, wondering if he'd written it for me. Then I'd jumped him in his apartment because I'd needed so badly to know he was real, to feel the real person in a way only I knew him. Travis had responded as he always did—with enthusiasm, with passion, with honest affection.

Here in this quiet car with just the two of us, with night falling outside, I could feel the complicated world falling away. I needed this. I needed him.

Travis is just a stop on the road. Make a plan.

Make an exit before things get messy.

No. Not now. I would put it off for a little longer. Right now I was on a road trip with my boyfriend to meet his parents. That was the only thing I wanted to think about. The only thing I *had* to think about. Everything else could wait.

"Do you remember when you drove from L.A. to Portland?" I asked him.

Travis nodded. The lights going by made beautiful shadows on his face. He hadn't shaved in a few days, and he had a rasp of beard on his jaw, which I had felt prickling against my skin a few hours ago. "I remember," he said.

"I was mad at myself for saying no," I confessed.

He grinned, and I felt the warmth of it in my whole body. "I knew it. Well, now you get a redo. Road trips with me are fun. Is that why you said yes when I suggested it? To make up for saying no?"

"I would have said yes to anything you suggested."

He glanced at me, something flickering behind those blue eyes before he turned his attention back to the road.

I watched him struggle silently, and then I said, "You're really trying not to say something filthy, aren't you?"

"It's a sacrifice," he admitted. "I can think of *so many* lines, all of them good. I can't pick one."

I felt myself smiling. "Make a list, then. I'll read it later."

He groaned. "Be careful what you ask for. My list is disgusting. Should we start at the top and go to the bottom, or should we start at the bottom and go to the top?"

That made me laugh. He had a talent for being funny and dirty at the same time. He was talented at other things, too. Maybe I'd make my own list.

Travis was smirking as he drove, but I thought that for a second I'd seen something serious in his expression when I'd said I would have done anything he suggested. That seriousness had vanished behind his dirty wit. I wondered whether I had imagined it. A moment of wishful thinking.

"I'm starving," I said. "Let's eat." I held up a hand before he could speak. "I'm not talking about sex, Travis. I'm talking about food."

"You're stifling my genius for depraved conversation," he complained. "But you win. Let's stop for dinner."

TRAVIS'S MOTHER WAS JANE—"CALL me Janey"—and his father was Ed. They lived in an RV that was currently in a park deep in Washington, far from the nearest interstate or big box store. Janey had long, graying hair that flowed down her back, and Ed had a tidy paunch and a bushy beard. They were textbook hippie types, and they were also flaky, interesting, and weird. I liked them immediately.

As Travis had predicted, Ed showed off the weed plant he was growing in a pot on the patio and gave me a detailed explanation of his cultivation process. "It takes *months* to grow weed," he said when I asked why the plant was in a pot instead of in the ground. "We don't stay anywhere long enough for a full cycle. It's the only thing I miss about having my own property and a yard."

Janey had made her granola bars—Travis obviously knew his parents very well—and she hugged me tight when we were introduced, a genuine squeeze that made me feel warm. When she pulled away, she patted my face gently, her eyes crinkling at the corners. "My goodness, you're beautiful," she said, and in that moment, I believed it.

We sat in lawn chairs around the campfire behind the RV and talked late into the night. Twenty years ago, Ed had invented a component used in microphones, had sold the patent, and retired. "It was enough for us," Ed said, gesturing expansively at the RV and the dark woods beyond. "I don't need more than this. Working a job sucks. As far as I'm concerned, I'm the richest man alive."

I glanced at Travis—who actually was rich, or had been. He didn't look like he had taken offense. He was sprawled in his battered lawn chair with a glass of his mother's hand-squeezed orange juice in his hand because his parents preferred weed and mushrooms to alcohol. He didn't look like a rock star here in the wilderness, wearing jeans and a plaid flannel shirt, his hair mussed, scruff on his jaw, the fire licking light over his face. He looked like he belonged here, and I could see clearly that even though he had ended up as the frontman for a world-famous band, this had been his life growing up. He rolled his eyes good-naturedly. "You just have to say it, don't you Dad?"

"You're rich, too, Trav." Ed gave him a pointed squint. "You have your health, your well-being, and now you have this lovely woman." He gestured to me. "You're the envy of any man on earth right now. What else do you need?"

"An apartment would be nice," Travis said. "A bank account. A job."

"The guy down the road pays ten bucks an hour to chop wood," Janey said helpfully. "Cash. And you could get plenty of money for that car."

Travis slapped a hand over his heart. "Not the car, Mom. Never the car."

"All right, then," she said. "There's a bar on the way into town that advertises live music on Saturday nights. Go talk to the manager and get the gig. Problem solved."

I sipped my drink, trying to figure out if she was joking. Was she actually suggesting that Travis White pick up a gig at a rural biker bar? No one was laughing, so maybe she was serious.

We'd taken a room at a motel half an hour's drive away, because even if we slept on the floor, there was no room for us to stay in the RV. Instead of rolling out sleeping bags in the dirt, we sprang the money for a dank room with bed linens like sandpaper and wispy thin towels. We crawled into bed late, both of us smelling of campfire, fully dressed against the room's chill. Travis pulled the polyester comforter over us and spooned behind me, snugging me into his heat.

"Okay, be honest," he said against my shoulder. "Did you hate it?"

"Of course not," I said in surprise. "Why would I hate it?"

"You're roughing it," he pointed out. "And my parents are weird."

"They're nice."

"Nice and weird."

I was getting used to this habit of his. Travis had a tendency to put himself down first, before anyone else could do it. It was a defense mechanism, and I wondered how he had gotten it, when he had gotten so hurt that he wanted to avoid it again. Did he think I would hurt him?

I stroked his forearm, running my fingers over the fine hairs. "I like them," I said firmly. "They're weird in the best way. They're very...you."

His body tensed against mine, almost a flinch, and then he held himself still. He didn't speak. He thought I might be insulting him, but he wasn't sure.

"What I mean is that I can see where you came from," I went on. "Not physically, but who you are. How you roll with things so easily, how you aren't hung up on material wealth."

He huffed a humorless laugh. "Katie, I owned a house in Malibu and five cars."

I stroked his forearm again. "Did you really lose everything?" I asked gently. Travis and I didn't talk about money very often.

"Maybe?" He phrased it as a question. "It's so fucking complicated, I don't even understand it. There's money I owe, money other people owe me, money that's supposed to be split among the band members but no one can agree on the percentages. There's money I never got paid, and then there's money I got paid but might owe back. My former agent owes me money, but I have to pay enormous lawyer fees to sue him for it. And on, and on." He sighed. "I made a mess of my career. If I'd met someone smart like you years ago, I might have avoided it, but money seemed like it was endless. For a long time, part of me couldn't believe I hadn't ended up playing a biker bar in rural Washington, so I just rode the wave."

"Was your mom really serious about that?" I asked.

"Sure she was. They know I got rich and famous, but that was never important to them. They don't listen to much pop music," he said wryly. "The way my parents see it, Dad made a bunch of money and used it to live the rest of his life the way he wanted to. They assumed I would do that, too. Just take a paycheck and use it to do something that mattered. Get a cabin in the woods, chop wood, and play country music on Saturday nights. That's their ideal life."

"It's so far away from Hollywood." I said it aloud almost by mistake as the thought drifted across my mind, half asleep.

"So far," he agreed. He rubbed his cheek against my shoulder through my T-shirt, as if reassuring himself that I was here. I was aware of him everywhere on my body, in every place he touched me, in the feel of his breath and the rise and fall of his chest, in his smell and the firmness of his arms. It wasn't about sex in the moment, but I let the idea drift pleasantly across my mind. I could roll over onto my back and pull him down to me. I could kiss his neck and run my hands under his shirt, and he would say yes. Even in this shabby room, on this terrible bed, it would be sleepy and slow and sweet.

Then I remembered Ed telling Travis that having me meant he was a rich man. And Stella advising me to plan our breakup.

I fell asleep wondering if I would ever know what to do.

TWENTY-FIVE

Travis

UNLIKE JANEY, Katie's mom liked to cook. She must have started from the moment Katie told her we were coming to visit, because by the time we got to the Armstrong home in Minneapolis, there was enough food for two Thanksgiving dinners laid out in the kitchen and the dining room. Since Katie and I had spent a day eating nothing but no-bake granola bars and airport food, my mouth watered when I walked through the door.

Katie had been wrong when she predicted that neither of her parents had heard of Seven Dog Down. Either she didn't know her parents' musical tastes or someone had tipped them off, because Liz—Katie's mom—was flushed and nervous when she introduced herself, and James—Katie's dad—pumped my hand and squeezed it with supernatural strength. Liz asked me four times in a row if the flight was all right, and James yanked my suitcase from my hand and carried it up the stairs to the room they'd made up for me.

Katie watched her parents ignore her as they fussed over me, and then she looked at me, her eyes narrowed.

I shrugged. "What did I do?"

Katie's lips pressed together. Just looking at her made me feel a little raw. I'd never brought a woman to meet my parents before, and the first one I'd introduced them to was a fake relationship. My parents hadn't helped with my campaign to get Katie to see me as real-boyfriend material. Katie and I would be lucky if we didn't get away from that motel with bedbugs.

"Scott," Katie said, nearly hissing the word.

I frowned. "Scott?"

"My brother." She gestured to where Liz was bringing a plate stacked with sliced ham from the kitchen. "He did this. He told them who you are."

"You didn't tell them who your boyfriend is?"

"I did, but you know what I mean. I bet Scott played them Seven Dog Down. Showed them YouTube clips of you. Now they know a celebrity is coming over."

"Katie, *you're* a celebrity."

"I don't count, and you know it."

I did know. If I was ever foolish enough to tell my parents to treat me like a celebrity, they would laugh in my face.

From the kitchen, we could hear Liz talking on her cell phone in the too-loud way of parents, as if they can't believe they don't need to shout. "Scott!" she bellowed. "They're here! They just got here! You told me to call you. Come over now!"

Katie showed me upstairs, where her parents had put her in her childhood bedroom and me in Scott's old bedroom down the hall. There would be no raunchy exploits in the Armstrong house. Katie's room had a double bed with a faded quilt on it.

My room was adorned with a stack of boxes next to the bed and a disused elliptical machine in the corner. It was a room that shouted, *My kid moved out and he's never coming back.*

It was all very nice, very normal. I was so nervous I thought I might throw up.

While Katie made a trip to the bathroom, I hid in my room and tried to breathe. What was I thinking, meeting her parents? Her brother? They expected Katie to meet a great guy, marry him, have kids. There was no universe in which they'd think that I was that guy. This was going to be a disaster, and we were stuck here for three days.

I could perform for a crowd—I was good at that. I could smile and wave at a group of fans and make them believe in the version of me they were looking at. But I had never spent three days with a girlfriend's parents. I suddenly didn't know how to act or what to say. What were we going to do for three days? Sit in the living room amongst plates of food and stare at each other?

I rummaged desperately through my bag and found a weed gummy in a side pocket. I popped it in my mouth before I could think better of it. I needed to take the edge off.

I rubbed my sweaty palms on my jeans as I listened to Katie leave the bathroom and go to her room.

Jesus, this was worse than being backstage at a sold-out arena. I didn't know what had come over me. It wasn't that I *didn't* want to get married—I had never thought about it. And kids? What rock star thinks about kids? Not me, though if Katie wanted kids, I was in. Should I say that if her parents asked me about kids? Katie and I had never talked about it, and by the way, our relationship was supposed to be fake, so why would we talk about kids? I was losing my mind.

"Are you all right?" Katie asked from my doorway, where

she was standing, watching me with a perplexed look on her face.

"Great." I straightened, dropping my hands from my jeans and trying to ignore the cold sweat breaking out all over my body. What if I got the nervous shits while I was here? There was only one bathroom in the upstairs hall. I'd have to make an excuse to leave the house and go in the bushes somewhere. Maybe if I did that, I'd just keep walking until I hit the Atlantic Ocean, then jump in and swim until no one remembered my humiliation.

Katie looked even more confused, but the front door slammed open and closed downstairs and Liz called out, "Come down, you two! Scott is here!"

Katie rolled her eyes. "I apologize in advance for my brother."

"Why? What's wrong with him?"

"He needs a personality transplant."

I blew out a breath. "Can you give me specifics? Will he beat me up? Do I have to listen to his political opinions? What am I dealing with here?"

"He's a know-it-all. He can debate even the stupidest topic for hours, so don't get him started. If he asks you inappropriate questions—which he will—don't answer them. Just follow my lead." She tilted her head, peering at me. "Are you sure you're okay?"

"Yeah, I'm swell." Weed gummies took too long to kick in. Their biggest drawback.

Scott was in the kitchen, briskly digging in to his mother's food. He was bearded and beefy, wearing jeans and a well-worn university sweatshirt. He gave me a narrow-eyed glare over the bite of ham he was chewing when we walked in. Katie had said that he had a wife and a kid, but there was no sign of either. It looked like he had left them at home so he could bust my balls with no distractions.

He grunted when I shook his hand, nodded at Katie, and turned his attention back to his plate. Were we expected to have a formal dinner, or were we just grazing from the mountain of food? I picked up a plate and held it, lost, until Katie nudged me. "Just eat," she prompted softly. "She'll be offended if you don't."

I put food on my plate and took a seat in the corner of the living room. This was Katie's family, Katie's show, and maybe everyone would pay attention to her and ignore me.

I had no such luck. For the next hour, Liz hovered over me, spooning more food onto my plate and asking questions—about how Katie and I met, about our vacation, about the visit to my parents. Scott sat down next to me, weirdly close, and interrupted my answers with comments. James cracked dad jokes. Katie, sitting at the table with her own plate, alternated between bailing me out of the hot seat and giving me amused smiles behind her family's backs. The gummy kicked in, and I floated, answering questions and thinking deep thoughts while I tried to pay attention.

Eventually, Scott—still giving me shifty eyes—said his goodbyes and left to go home to his mythical family. Katie helped her parents clean up in the kitchen, and when I tried to pitch in, Liz kept shooing me to a chair. The Armstrongs talked about relatives, neighbors, people Katie had gone to school with, the chatter flowing over me as I sat in my chair, wondering if I was coming across as stupid, aloof, or both. Maybe neither. It was clear I had no idea how to do this boyfriend thing.

Night had fallen outside, and the Armstrong parents turned on *Dateline* on the living room TV. Katie sat with them, talking quietly. The dishwasher hummed in the kitchen and the clock ticked in the hall. It felt normal. This was what Katie had come from, the foundation of who she was. She was a Hollywood actress now, but she had once been a kid doing her homework in her room in this same house while her parents watched TV with her brother down the hall. This house was why she was still so grounded and kind in the chaos of show business. I wondered what would have happened if teenaged Katie had met teenaged Travis, who was planning to escape his hippie parents by joining a band. If we had met then, she wouldn't have gotten her homework done, that much was sure. But it would have been fun.

I took a hot shower in the bathroom upstairs, then maneuvered around the elliptical in my room to dress for bed. When I came out of the bathroom after brushing my teeth, the TV was still on downstairs, but the door to Katie's bedroom creaked open as if she had been waiting for me. She waved me in.

She had dressed for bed, too. She closed the door softly behind me and we tiptoed into her bed, pulling the quilt over us. I snugged my knees behind hers and felt her back warm my front. "This feels like it's against the rules," I whispered in her ear, even though we were fully dressed and we were both in our thirties.

"It is. It definitely is." I heard the smile in Katie's voice. She leaned back and looked at me. "You hate rules."

"I'm in my element," I admitted, kissing her softly.

"Right. So, do you hate my parents?"

"No."

"Good. I know it was awkward. They'll get used to you, I promise."

I looked into her face, and suddenly I knew that I *could* do this. I could come back to this house for Christmases and long summer weekends. I could eat Liz's cooking and listen to James's dad jokes. I could win over Scott and meet his missing wife and kid. I could learn who all the relatives were and get used to the elliptical. I could be Katie's boyfriend, and not only would I be good at it, I would love it. If what we had was real.

Katie's expression had gone serious. Maybe she was thinking about the words she'd just said—that her parents would get used to me, as if we were a couple who would see her parents from now on. I watched her thinking, and words tumbled over themselves in my throat. *Throw the script out. Be my girlfriend. Do you want kids? If you don't, it's cool. But what if you did? Would you have them with me?*

Maybe I was crazy or high. I was definitely impulsive. It was probably a bad idea to say any of those things. I had never said them to any other woman. But bad ideas were my favorite kind, and maybe I should say all of it to *this* woman. If I didn't ask, how would I ever know her answer?

Before I could open my chest and pour everything out to her, Katie pulled me down and kissed me, long and deep. She was warm against me under the quilt, and then we were making out, her hands smoothing down my back. I should stop this and tell her that I'd wait for her while she shot her movie in Budapest, that we should get married. Any minute now, I would.

Katie froze and pushed me away, her eyes going wide. "Listen," she hissed in a panicked whisper.

I couldn't hear anything but the blood rushing in my ears. "What?" I whispered back.

"They turned the TV off." Footsteps creaked downstairs, then moved to the staircase. "They're going to bed."

One set of footsteps—James's—moved past our door down the hall. Liz's steps followed more softly. "Katie?" she called out. "Your light is on. Are you awake?"

"Oh no, no, no," Katie whispered as she shoved me. "Get off."

"You can't be serious," I whispered back. "We're adults. We aren't even naked."

"I can't help it. I feel like I'm fourteen. Hurry!" She shoved me again.

I rolled to the edge of the bed—just as the doorknob turned and the bedroom door swung open.

TWENTY-SIX

Katie

MOM SMILED at me as she peeked around the door. "Oh, good," she said. "You're awake. I thought you might be."

I smiled back, smoothing the covers down on my bed. "Mom, it's only ten o'clock."

"True. I guess we keep early hours compared to what you're used to."

My parents still thought that my life involved a lot more partying than it actually did. I had explained to them about long shooting hours and early calls. I'd brought them to visit me in L.A. only twice over the years, because every other time I'd offered, I had been turned down. Neither of my parents had seemed happy when I brought them to Hollywood. They had been bewildered, as if they weren't sure why they were in such a strange place and only wanted to go home.

I loved my parents, but there was an essential piece of me

that they didn't understand and never would. Ever since I had first seen *The Wizard of Oz* on TV as a kid, I had wanted to be an actress. I had wanted to play Dorothy and make magic on a yellow brick road. I'd been willing to work hard to make that happen, first by joining theater club at school, then begging my parents for acting and dancing lessons. I'd modeled, taken bit parts, and worked as an extra—anything that would get me onto a set and in front of a camera.

I didn't do it for attention—I did it because acting made me happy and because I was good at it. Through acting, I could lead dozens of lives, hundreds even, instead of one. I could tell stories and make people feel things. Going to Hollywood had seemed like success, and it was, but it also meant I had to work even harder than before.

But part of me was still a Minnesota girl. The people in Hollywood didn't understand my Minnesota side, and the people in Minnesota didn't understand my Hollywood side. I was starting to suspect that the only person who could fully understand both was the man who was currently hiding under the bed, where he'd rolled just as Mom opened the door.

I shifted on the bed, silently pleading with him to stay quiet. It shouldn't have mattered so much that Travis was in my room—he was right about that—but it did. I would unpack it some other time. In the meantime, Mom crossed the room and sat on the edge of the bed, taking my hand and patting it.

"It's so nice to have you home, honey," she said. "I love it when you visit."

I squeezed her hand and swallowed hard. The old sadness came over me—the feeling that the real me lived both here and in L.A., and nothing I ever did would make the two sides come together. I would always be turning my back on one or the other. "Thanks, Mom."

"And you brought a boyfriend. You've never done that before."

I had never brought Jeremy to meet my parents, even though we had dated for a year. Something had always come up. Jeremy had never been interested in my Minnesota life. Travis had jumped at the chance to see it.

I pictured Travis under the bed, with a good view of Mom's ankles as he listened in. "Um, right," I said.

"I like him." Mom squeezed my hand, and I realized that this conversation was the reason she had come in here. She wanted to talk about Travis.

"That's great," I said, cutting her off. "Okay, then, I think—"

"He's sweet," Mom continued, as if I had asked for her opinion. "He was a little high, I think."

Oops. I should have known Mom would catch that. Travis had been so polite and spacey that I had caught on right away. He must have had a gummy in one of his pockets. "He doesn't do that often," I rushed to explain. "I think he was just nervous."

"I don't know why," Mom said. "He's very famous. Still, it gave him an appetite. I refilled his plate three times."

"Great," I said. "Okay, well—"

"He likes you," Mom went on. "I can tell from the way he looked at you. Scott said that you two are all over the internet lately, so I was worried that he's shallow. But even though I just met him, I don't think he is."

No, Travis wasn't shallow. He just pretended to be, and very effectively, too. "Travis isn't shallow," I said clearly enough for him to hear. "He's very smart."

Mom gave a skeptical blink. "What matters is that he's nice to you," she said noncommittally.

"He's nice to me," I said, enunciating so that he could hear me under the bed. I had never regretted anything in my life more than shoving Travis under the bed. If Mom had come in to find Travis in bed with me, we wouldn't be having this awkward conversation. I really needed to get over my good-girl instincts sometime. "Travis is a great boyfriend," I said.

"I just like to see you having fun for once," Mom said. "That's what I came in here to say. You've always been so serious and so driven, ever since you first discovered acting. You never took time to explore or act out, like most young people do. You've been the same with boyfriends—you either date someone seriously, or you don't date at all. It's nice to see you just have fun with someone, even if it's just for a little while."

I stared at her. Mom thought I didn't have fun? Okay, she was mostly right. But she thought Travis was nothing but a bit of fun. And she thought we were—

"What do you mean, *just for a little while?*" I asked.

"Everything doesn't have to be so serious," Mom said, patting my knee. "Even in relationships before you settle down. Travis is showing you that, and I'm grateful for it. Having fun with a man like Travis is something every girl needs at least once in her life. He reminds me of the college boyfriend I had before I met your father. He wasn't husband material, but he was *something*. And by the time James came along, I knew what husband material looked like, and that's what I wanted."

"Mom, please." Travis was *hearing* this. Hearing my mother talk about him as if he was a short-term fling. It was getting worse by the minute. "This is awkward. We need to change the subject."

She waved me off. "I know you don't want to talk to me about this stuff, but I'm right. If I could pick a man to show you a good time for once, it would be Travis. He's perfect." She gave me a sidelong look. "He's easy on the eyes, too. Not just the front, but the back."

"Mom, stop." I nearly shouted it. I grabbed the bedcovers and pulled them halfway over my face. "Stop."

"I'm just saying, good lord." She grinned, enjoying my embarrassment. "The way he walks—I saw you looking. I bet you're sorry we put you two in separate bedrooms."

"*Stop.* Please."

She laughed, then stood and walked to the door. "Night, honey." She closed the door behind her.

Under the bed, Travis cleared his throat. I heard shuffling as he maneuvered himself out of there.

I dropped the blanket and watched him unfold from the floor, brushing dust off of his sleep pants. "That wasn't great," he admitted. "At all."

"I'm sorry." I flung off the bedclothes and stood to help him brush off. "I'm so sorry. You shouldn't have listened to me. We should have just embarrassed her. I was totally wrong."

"I'm actually impressed at how clean it was under there." He swiped his hands through his hair. "Still, I'd rather not know that your mom clocked my ass. Also that she figured out the weed. I'm sorry about that. I've never met a girlfriend's parents before, and I didn't want to say the wrong thing and come off like an asshole."

"She isn't usually like that," I said. "She's never talked like that about someone I'm dating before. I don't know what came over her."

Travis's gaze skated away from mine and moved around the room, focusing on nothing. He was covering it, but his feelings were hurt—probably at my mother implying that he was stupid or calling him a short-term fling. Everything had been going so well. What was wrong with people?

The silence got thicker, heavier, and I had the instinct to

pretend this wasn't happening. I could change the subject or kiss him, and we wouldn't talk about it, and we'd carry on with this visit as if everything was fine. I couldn't stand that idea. The look in his eyes ripped my heart out.

"Travis," I said, "please don't listen to my mother's stupid opinions. She doesn't know you."

He nodded, still not looking at me, and then he winced as if he was thinking something harsh.

"Yeah," he said. "It's cool."

"Travis, look at me."

He turned those blue eyes to me, and there was so much happening behind them that I couldn't name it all. He focused on my face, and his eyebrows twitched down in a frown. He was working up to something.

"I don't think we should break up," he said. He took a breath. "You know—yet."

I stepped closer to him. "Neither do I." I put my hand on his wrist, needing to feel how solid he was, how real. "Stella thinks we should," I admitted.

Travis nodded. "So does Jonathan."

"What?" I was offended, even though Stella had said the same thing to me. "Excuse me? Why does Jonathan think we should break up?"

"Because of the tour, and you going to Budapest, and once you've shot with Edgar Pinsent, you'll have a lot of offers." Travis dropped his gaze. "He says that celebrity relationships are the hardest to manage, mostly because of the schedules. He says they almost never work out, so it's best to manage the breakup instead of being surprised by it."

That was so exactly what Stella had said to me that I wondered if our agents had talked about it behind our backs. I wouldn't put it past either of them. I had a secret suspicion that

Stella and Jonathan were hooking up. I would deal with that later.

"Everything is so confusing," I said, keeping hold of Travis's wrist. "I don't know what's real and what isn't. I don't know what's just for the cameras or the internet or our agents or our parents, and I don't know what's just us."

Travis looked around the room. "Katie, none of those people are here. No one is watching. There are no cameras. There's only us in this room." He swallowed. "And I don't want to break up."

I stepped close to him, sliding my hand down his wrist to his hand and clasping it in mine. "Neither do I," I told him. "So we don't break up. You're right—there's no one here. We write this script, Travis. Together. We don't want to write the ending yet. So we won't."

His hand unfolded against mine, and as his eyes met mine, his fingers gripped me back. "It'll be difficult," he said, though there was hope in his voice. "We'll be apart."

"So we'll talk," I said. "Often."

"We'll be in different time zones. And Edgar Pinsent might not want you talking to me while you're shooting."

"He can't control who I talk to," I said. "He's a director, not my jailer. If I have to get a top-secret burner phone to talk to you, then I will."

Travis stepped in so that his body was lightly pressed to mine, his warmth against my skin through our clothes. "You'll meet some prestigious Oscar-winning actor, and he'll ask you to run away with him," he said in that Travis way of his, flippant and anxious at the same time.

"Will I? Then I guess he'll be disappointed," I said. "I can resist Mr. Gravitas if you can resist half-dressed groupies."

Travis rolled his eyes. "Please." And I believed him. It was crazy, but I did, just like he believed me. It was a leap of faith—and it felt good.

I tilted my chin up and brushed my lips over his. "So we agree. No ending yet," I said against his skin.

He let out a soft breath. "No ending yet," he agreed, and he kissed me.

TWENTY-SEVEN

Travis

WHEN I WAS EIGHTEEN, I thought that being onstage in front of a crowd was better than anything else I could experience. Better than food, better than sex, maybe even better than love, if I knew what that was. Sweating under the lights with my band behind me, inhaling air heavy with sweat and stale beer, hearing a crowd sing along or shout my name—that was what it meant to feel alive, and in my world, nothing else came close.

Now, years later, as I stood in front of a crowd for the first time in a long time, sweating through my clothes and riding a wall of sound, I thought my teenaged self might have been right.

I had been so used to this at one time. Being on back-to-back tours had almost made this routine, something I did as a job, one I was good at. The cliché of the rock star who can't remember what city he's in is very close to the truth. The exhaustion and the repetition made me numb after a while, and the shitty bandmates and subpar music I was saddled with didn't help. For a time, before it all fell down, I forgot that being a rock star was fun.

Then I wasn't a rock star anymore, and when I was curled up on a sofa with tea towels swaddling my hands, I still forgot.

I remembered it now.

Seven thousand people packed this place—not to see me, but to see the Road Kings. The Road Kings were playing a sold-out show in Seattle, and in true Road Kings fashion, they were nice enough to add me to the bill and asshole enough to make me their opening act. The Road Kings were famous for *never* booking an opening act. They made an exception for me.

It was payback for the glitter bomb, of course. It was also payback for all the times I'd shit talked them over the years, for being a sellout for a while, and—according to Stone Zeeland— "for being an annoying punk." Which—okay, fair. It was humbling. It was also an opportunity to get in front of a sold-out crowd with songs I'd written and give them a taste of the new album just as it released. It was an opportunity. A bet. And like I'd told Denver, if you bet against me, you'll lose.

I thought I'd be nervous, but that was only for a brief moment. Then I remembered that I was born to do this and nothing else. I went out onstage with my new band and played the songs I'd written—good songs. A wave of approval lifted when the lights came on, and in that first second, I felt a familiar spark. This crowd hadn't come here just for me, but they were happy I was on the bill. They wanted to see Travis White. They had missed me. I could taste their anticipation. Every thought of being nervous evaporated. This crowd was on the edge of its seat, waiting, and before I played the first note, I had them in the palm of my hand.

Then we played our set, and we killed it.

The Road Kings had only given us thirty minutes, and we made every minute count. I hooked the crowd. I drew them in. I got them dancing. I made them laugh. It was hard, but it was also easy. The crowd wanted to like me, so I let them. I also gave them good music. Sometimes it doesn't need to be more complicated than that.

Denver fist bumped me backstage, and Stone thumped me on the back, maybe a little harder than necessary. Sienna was there in her professional capacity, because as we'd agreed, she had an exclusive. It felt great, but suddenly I needed to sit alone in my dressing room for a minute as the Road Kings went onstage.

I closed the door behind me, sat down, and put my head between my knees, wondering curiously what I was about to do. Pass out? Puke? Cry? Nothing yet. I waited, trying to let my feelings happen the way they tell you to in self-help YouTube videos. Was I emotional about all of this? How was I supposed to know?

The only thing I could think in that moment was that I wished Katie was here. I wished she had seen that I could do it. If she were here, she would say that she already knew that. But still, I wished she had seen.

She had been in L.A. while I did my final rehearsals, and now she was in London for her meeting with Edgar Pinsent. We were starting the careers that would take us away from each other. We talked every day, but I hadn't seen her in weeks.

We had finished the visit with her parents without any more embarrassment. I made nice with the Armstrongs, stayed out of Katie's bedroom, and tried not to think about that fact that even her mom—who hadn't known who I was until Scott filled her in—thought we wouldn't last. I could deal with some lady in Minnesota thinking I wasn't good boyfriend material.

I'd add her to the list of people I needed to prove wrong, as long as Katie and I stuck it out.

The tour was scheduled now that the album had released, and the dates lined up that I'd likely be leaving while Katie was shooting in Budapest. When she was done with filming, she could either come see me on tour or wait for me in L.A. while she lined up more work. I rented a house in L.A., but I didn't plan to be there much, and I didn't know how long I would live there. If the album and the tour both tanked, I would probably be adrift again.

As I was pondering all of this with my head between my knees—it was a lot—my phone rang.

I didn't recognize the number, but very few people had this number, so I picked up. It could be Katie calling from London.

"Hello?" I said.

"Mr. White." The man's voice was unfamiliar. "This is Edward Glee."

I frowned at the floor. I had never heard that name before, and I would remember if I had. The first thing I thought was that this man, whoever he was, should get into voice acting, because though I didn't know what he looked like, he sounded like Morgan Freeman.

The man seemed to be awaiting an answer, so I said, "Do I know you, Edward Glee?"

"You know my assistants, Mr. White. Though actually you don't, because you've been avoiding their calls and correspondence admirably. I am your lawyer."

"I already have a lawyer." More than one.

"I'm your new lawyer," Edward Glee said in his sonorous voice. I expected him to start talking about breaking out of Shawshank. "Your old lawyer retired, and I took over his cases. Or didn't you read those letters, either?"

I sighed, feeling the high of the show draining away. It had been such a good night, and now I had my reminder that I *needed* to succeed because of my fucked-up financial situation. "Look, man," I said as calmly as I could, "I'm sure you're a nice guy, but I'm backstage at a show right now, and this isn't a good time, and—Wait, why are you calling so late? It's way past business hours."

"I'm calling now," Edward Glee said, "because my assistants have been chasing you for weeks, and you haven't responded. You're excellent at avoidance, Mr. White. But the situation has become critical, so I decided to contact you myself. I thought that getting you in the evening would give me better chances."

I stared at the floor between my feet, willing a chasm to appear so I could fall in and avoid this conversation. I should have just hung up. But I had never talked to this man before, and something in his voice said that he was confident I needed to hear him. Besides, who hangs up on Morgan Freeman?

"Mr. Glee," I said, "You're trying to help, but I don't need to go over my situation again. I know how permanently fucked up it is. I can pay your bills, but not if they're astronomically high. I should warn you about that up front. You might want to get yourself a richer client."

"Mr. White," Glee retorted, "As your lawyer, I would appreciate it if you would let me make my own assessment about wasting my valuable time. I can also assess whether your situation is indeed fucked up, as you put it. Please stop talking and listen."

That shut me up. "Fine. Go ahead."

"I'll skip over much of the uninteresting legal details and cut to the chase. When I took over, the first thing I did was read over the contract you originally signed. Please answer me one question honestly. How old were you when you signed that first contract?"

"Twenty."

"And that age is reflected in the contract?"

I scratched the back of my neck. Why was he asking me this if he was the one reading the contract? "I guess so."

"You *guess*, Mr. White. Guessing has lost many a legal case."

My head was starting to hurt. It always felt like this, talking about my situation. It was why I had given up and started avoiding it. "Okay, I was twenty. Why is that important?"

"It's important because two months before you signed that contract, the company implemented a rule that they cannot sign anyone under twenty-one without additional parental or legal consent."

I stared at the floor, which started to waver and swirl. "Say again?"

"The company had several lawsuits that came from signing minors, so they instituted new protections. Anyone under twenty-one had to have a parent or legal representative cosign the contract. I'm looking at that contract right now. You were twenty. And no one else signed with you."

Of course no one else had signed it. I had been a kid offered his dream of fame, not a guy with a lawyer on retainer. No one had told me that I needed someone in authority to help me sign my life away, because that's how you rope in gullible musicians when you tell them you're going to make them famous.

My problem stemmed all the way back to the day I signed that contract, and now here I was. Throwing the dice on a final hope of having the kind of success I had wanted since I was fifteen. Sacrificing my pride, my reputation, and time with the girl I loved to make it happen. All because I had been impulsive and stupid.

"So I screwed up by signing it," I said as red clouded my

vision. I was becoming chokingly angry, though I didn't know at who. Myself. Them. Everyone.

But what Edward said next put me in a spin again. "No, Mr. White. They screwed up by offering you that contract in the first place. There's a reason that rules came into place about signing minors. Signing minors means that kids like you get taken advantage of—situations exactly like the one you find yourself in. They had put the new rule in place, but they still signed you, either by mistake or with ill intent. It doesn't matter which. The terms of the contract were null and void in the first place. Legally, the entire contract I have in front of me is trash."

I closed my eyes. "Mr. Glee, man, I'm begging you. Knock off the mystifying wordage and give me some good news for once. After all that, please don't say that I'm even more screwed than I was before."

My lawyer sighed. "Again, I'll keep it brief." A lie, I already knew. "What's going to happen is that we will file a lawsuit. There will be a lot of back and forth, as you can imagine, which you will let me handle. But they don't have a legal leg to stand on, so in the end, we'll settle. And when we do, I will make sure you are paid every dollar your twenty-year-old self is owed, plus a great deal extra to cover my time. But even after you've settled my bills, Mr. White, you will be a very, very rich man. Richer than you can imagine. That much, I can tell you. That much, I'm more sure of than I've ever been of anything in my life."

I thought of my old house being sold, the guys from the designers taking my shoes away. Living at Andy's. Borrowing money to buy a guitar. My mom suggesting that I play at a local bar for a few drinks and a few dollars.

I put my head in my hand. And I started to laugh.

TWENTY-EIGHT

Katie

EDGAR PINSENT DIDN'T MEET me in an office or a studio. He met me in a house overlooking Hampstead Heath, the kind of place that belonged on *Bridgerton* and had probably housed a duke sometime in the last four hundred years. The duke would have been handsome, of course. And single. Dark and tortured, yet secretly yearning for love. I needed to read fewer romance novels.

Though Edgar was American—he was born in Chicago, according to my googling—he didn't look out of place here. He sat behind a desk in a beautiful office with deep wood floors and an honest-to-god tapestry on the wall. I remembered what year it was when I saw that he was wearing a hip T-shirt under a blazer along with cowboy boots and jeans. He was forty-three —again, according to my googling—and the only thing that made him look English was his pasty complexion that hadn't seen much sunlight.

One of his assistants, Rita, had shown me into the office, and she stood next to his chair, a little like a servant would. It was weird, but I tried to ignore it as I shook Edgar's hand and sat down across from him.

"So you want to work on the film," Edgar said, crossing one ankle over his other knee and regarding me with seriousness.

This was it. My big chance. I had done my research, so I knew that Edgar Pinsent didn't like too much flattery because he didn't like fakes. So I said, "I'd be really excited to do it, if that's what's in the cards."

"Maybe," Edgar said. "I have something in mind. Do you want something to drink? Tea? The English love their tea. I think we have some."

"I'm fine." I looked around. "Is this *your* house?"

Edgar gave a tight shrug. "When I'm in London. I haven't been here much, because I've been working on the script."

I nodded. "Sure. The script. As my agent likely told you, I'd love to read—"

"No." He cut me off firmly. "You won't be reading the script. Not until we begin final prep."

I stared at him. "I can't...read the script?"

"It's how I work," Edgar said, as Rita stood there unmoving. What was she doing here? "I don't like everyone reading the script and imprinting their voices over mine. I need the actor's raw reactions to what I've written, not rehearsed moves. I need it to be real."

It made no sense. Who made a movie without reading the script? An actor needed to rehearse lines, to work scenes with their scene partners. We needed to learn blocking. And what about prep for action scenes, fight scenes, or—god forbid—sex scenes? How was I supposed to do everything blind? "Is this how you've always worked?" I asked him. "I haven't heard—"

"I use the method that works best for the project, whatever

that may be," Edgar said. "This is how this project cries out to be created."

I forced myself to keep still and not glance around the room to check if I was being pranked. "Mr. Pinsent, I need some kind of details. I have to be able to prepare."

"I'll explain what your role is," he replied. "As for preparation, I'll let you know what you need to do. It will be a three-month shoot, and the cast and crew will be secluded for that time. That means no visits home, and no one visiting you. The isolation will feed your creativity."

I nodded, but for the first time I thought that this setup was too close to a murder mystery setup for comfort. Maybe ten actors would go to the shoot, but only nine would come back. Or we'd get picked off one by one. Or this was all an elaborate psychological experiment, and we were—

"You'll also need to lose twenty-five pounds," Edgar said.

I blinked. "I beg your pardon?"

"Twenty-five should do it." His gaze flicked down, over my jeans and blameless cardigan. I thought I looked nice. "I'd prefer thirty, if you can manage it, but I realize that the timeline is tight."

"Twenty-five pounds? Is my character stranded on an island? Starving?"

Edgar ignored the question, though Rita gave me a sour look. "No cosmetic procedures are allowed before the shoot. Whatever Botox you're getting, it stops now. No lifts or tucks. I need your face to look real."

I scowled at him. "Hey." You do *not* discuss a lady's Botox unless you're her doctor or her husband. "That's presumptuous."

"It's necessary," Edgar countered. "I'd like you to work with a trainer so that your body is toned. Also, I'm not on social media myself, but Rita tells me that you've been in the tabloids lately with a famous boyfriend. That has to stop."

I did look around then, wondering if someone was joking. All of that careful planning for the past few months, my elaborate scheme, the script. All of it to get Edgar Pinsent's attention and make him think I was more than just a romcom girl, that I was a woman with depth. All to give him a glimpse of a personality that I had thought he would like.

The weeks with Travis, our planning of Instagram posts, the way we'd both walked a line we didn't understand. We had played pretend instead of actually dating, instead of letting ourselves fall in love, and we had done all of it for this man in this moment.

He had just dismissed all of it by basically saying he thought it was stupid. All of it.

"Why on earth," I said slowly, "would you need me to break up with my boyfriend in order to shoot a movie?"

"I don't want bad publicity around my project," Edgar said with a shrug, casually suggesting I end the best relationship in my life and break Travis's heart. "Tabloid publicity is bad publicity."

"It isn't a tabloid." What year was he living in? "It's the internet. And I haven't done anything that has bad publicity. Travis and I are both single, and we're dating. What's wrong with two people dating?"

"He's some kind of famous musician," Edgar said. I had so carefully cast Travis as my boyfriend, and Edgar had never heard of him. "Bad publicity always follows musicians around, and you're too exposed while you're with him." He shrugged again, as if he wasn't sure why we were spending so much time discussing this. "Get rid of him. It's a hard condition. I make art, not media circuses. He should be gone by the time we start final prep in a few weeks."

"No," I said.

There was a moment of stunned silence in the room. "Pardon?" Edgar said.

"No." I was sweating and rigid with nerves, but I was also starting to get angry. "I'm not breaking up with my boyfriend for this role. The star of your last movie got divorced because he slept with the nanny. Why didn't you care about *his* bad publicity?"

"Are you saying you don't want the part?" Edgar's eyebrows rose. "You're replaceable."

"Who are you going to replace me with who meets your morality standards? A nun?"

Rita let out a whispered gasp that told me that no one talked to Edgar Pinsent like this. Maybe I was torching my career, but I noticed that Edgar had avoided answering my question. I had the feeling that the morality rules only applied to actresses, not actors.

"My films are art," Edgar said, his face going red. "I'm offering you the chance of a lifetime. By the way, it will be the easiest money you've ever made. All you need to do is lie still on a mortuary slab, and your career will never be the same."

I gasped at that, louder than Rita had. "The role is a dead body? Are you serious? You want me to give up thirty pounds, three months of my life, and my boyfriend to play a *dead body*?"

"It's central to the plot," he argued. "The hero has to avenge your murder."

"My murder is naked? Is that necessary?"

"It's central to the plot," he argued again.

I pushed my chair back and stood. I was angry now. Who did he think he was? "You have no idea," I said, "*no idea* what I've done to get this meeting. How I've upended not only my life, but other people's lives. I've said no to other projects—ones that paid. I made a thriller. Did you even see it?"

"I have no idea what you're talking about."

So he hadn't seen *Honor Student*, which I'd made to impress him. I'd picked it so carefully.

"You're missing out," I snapped. "It's a good movie. I've shown my talent and my range. I've auditioned over and over. I traveled all the way here. And all you want is someone who is skinny, naked, and dead."

"In a great film," Edgar spat. "It's either that or more romcoms."

"I like romcoms. That's why I make them. And you aren't my only option to do other things. I'm already expanding without your help. I don't need to play dead to have a career."

He was flushed, though he kept his voice calm. "So you're saying no."

"I won't be going to your weird serial-killer shoot, no. I'll be busy doing other projects. Ones in which I'm alive."

They both stared at me, and the moment felt over. Like the end of a good scene. So I turned and walked out of the room.

No one stopped me.

That was a great exit, I thought as I walked onto the street and called an Uber. *I'll have to write that one down.*

TWENTY-NINE

Katie

TRAVIS WASN'T ANSWERING his phone. I tried repeatedly, but when it defaulted to voice mail, I had to do a calculation of what time it was on the US west coast. I was too frazzled to figure it out, so I gave up.

I had planned to be here for a few days, working out the details with Edgar and (I thought) reading the script, but when I got back to my hotel, I changed my mind. I packed, checked out, and got back into an Uber on the way to Heathrow airport. In the car, I tried Travis again. He didn't pick up, so I left a voicemail.

"Hey," I said to the recording. "I'm coming home early. It didn't work out with Edgar, but I'm fine—it's a long story. I'll tell you everything when I talk to you. Where are you, anyway? You always pick up. I'm going to the airport now to change my ticket and get on a flight. I'll see you when I get home, I guess. If you get this in time, call me back." I paused, because I wanted to tell him I loved him. But saying it for the first time in a voicemail was lame, so instead I said, "Okay, bye," which was deeply unsatisfying. I hung up.

My phone stayed silent as I arrived at the airport, navigated my way through with my bag, and stood in line at the airline counter. It stayed silent as I moved toward the front of the line. The man in front of me was finishing up when my phone finally rang. It was Travis.

"Katie?" He sounded breathless when I answered. "Where are you?"

"I'm at the airport, getting on a flight," I replied. "Where are you?"

"Don't get on a flight!" he said, panicked. "Don't go anywhere!"

"Why not?"

"Because I'm here."

I looked around. "Where?"

"In London. At Heathrow. I just landed."

My heart leapt in surprised joy. I hadn't thought I could feel so happy so quickly. "You came to London?"

He was panting as if he was jogging. "I wanted to surprise you. I just got off the flight."

"Ma'am?" The airline agent was waiting for me, uninterested in my mental state.

"Sorry," I said to her, then ducked out of the line, maneuvering my bag and the phone at the same time. I dropped into a wildly uncomfortable plastic chair as people moved past. "Travis, why did you come to London?"

"I had to see you," he said. "I got some news. Incredible news. It got me thinking, and now I'm full of ideas, and I didn't want to call you. I wanted to talk to you in person, and then I thought I should be there anyway to be your moral support while you get the role with Pinsent, and we can go celebrate together. I thought, Why the hell not? So I got on a plane."

"Oh." My throat closed. I had never had anyone in my corner like Travis, and it felt so good. "That's so sweet. I have news, too."

"I got your voicemail. What's going on? Wait, we shouldn't do this on the phone. Where exactly are you?"

I told him, and he told me where he was, and we coordinated our way through the enormous maze that is Heathrow airport. I spent forty-five minutes with my bag in one hand and my phone to my ear, running frazzled through corridors and food courts as Travis came through Customs and did the same. It was confusing and frustrating, and it wasn't *Love, Actually*—but I hated that movie, so I didn't mind.

When I finally caught sight of Travis standing outside the doors near a taxi stand, I said "There you are!" then hung up my phone and broke into a run. I watched him swivel, his phone still held up. Even though he wore a hoodie and a ball cap, I would know him anywhere. I had no idea whether anyone had recognized either of us, and I didn't care.

Travis saw me coming. He slung his bag over his shoulder and jogged toward me, his expression lighting up. "Watch it!" someone griped as he bumped past them. A cabbie tried to wave him over for a fare. Cars honked as he jogged across the pavement. And then I flung myself at him and was in his arms.

I felt his arms tighten around my middle and lift me off my feet as I buried my face in his neck. There was more honking, and someone else shouted, but I didn't care. I felt Travis's chest shake with quiet laughter as he put me down. "Hey, sweetheart," he said in that low voice in my ear. "It's been a while."

I pulled back just enough to kiss him soundly on the mouth. "I have so much to tell you," I said. "I couldn't wait."

"Same," he said. I looked into those blue eyes and I could

see how happy he was, truly happy to see me. To be with me. It wasn't a show. I was starting to think it never had been.

We talked at the same time. I said, "Listen, we should—"

"I have to—"

"It's—"

"You go first."

"No, you."

We smiled at each other. Airport security gave us increasingly hostile looks. People bumped past us, annoyed. Travis tilted my chin up and kissed me again. I remembered the first time he'd ever kissed me in an airport, and all of the times after. It had never been a show for me, either.

"Where are we going?" he asked me when he broke the kiss. "London or L.A.?"

"Travis! You just got off a plane. You can't turn around and fly back."

"I will if that's what you want to do."

"I checked out of my hotel," I said. "I could call them and get us back in. If they won't take us, we'll find somewhere else to stay."

"We'll figure it out," Travis said in that confident way of his that said he could wing anything. "You want to stay in London and have fun for a few days before going home?"

"I want to be where you are," I said, and I watched his face light up even more. "And you're here."

"Look out, London," Travis said, hailing us a cab.

I didn't know where we were going. It didn't matter. I already knew it would be somewhere good.

THIRTY

Travis

"HE WANTED YOU TO PLAY WHAT?" I asked.

Katie poked at her martini with the swizzle stick, then took a deep swig. We were sitting in the bar of the hotel she'd left, which had taken her back. They had given us a secluded, shadowed table in a corner. We were both too worn out to go out on the town, and besides, we needed to talk. I had taken a shower and changed, so at least I wasn't airplane-grimy for this conversation.

"You heard me," Katie said. Her cheeks were flushed, partly from the martini and partly from outrage. Wisps of her hair were falling out of the hairdo she'd made when she twisted it back off her face. She looked wildly beautiful, untouchable, unstoppable, and she had no idea.

I took a sip of my wine. "He wanted you to play dead."

"And naked," Katie added. "Don't forget that."

I cleared my throat. I looked around the room. I ran a hand through my hair. I cleared my throat again.

"Travis, you're a terrible actor. I can tell you're trying not to laugh."

"Um." I winced. "I'm sorry. But it's at least a little bit funny?" I held my thumb and finger an inch apart. "A tiny bit? Enraging. But funny."

"I turned down Edgar Pinsent after chasing him for months." Katie looked down into her drink. "It felt so right at the time, but is my career over? He was truly offering me the role. Am I the asshole?"

"Katie," I said, "you are so, so much better than that. On your lowest day, you're better than that. It was a dick offer. From a dick."

She stirred her drink again. "I haven't had the guts to call Stella. Will she fire me?"

"Stella will fly here to put the heel of her stiletto in Edgar Pinsent's eye for suggesting her client lose twenty-five pounds and give up three months to be in one shot as a dead body. Then she'll send you five more scripts and tell you to pick one."

I watched her shoulders go down, not entirely but enough. "I was so mad," she said after a moment of silence. "So mad. I worked so hard and did so much, and when I finally got there, he really did look at me like a piece of meat. Like I didn't matter at all. When he told me to break up with you to get the role, I knew I couldn't do it."

"Wait." I didn't think I had heard her right. "He told you what?"

"He said I had to break up with you to get the role." She made a face. "*Get rid of him* are the words he used. Like he had a right to run my personal life. God, it was infuriating."

"Hold on." I held up a hand, slow on the uptake. "You're saying that after everything we did to get his attention, it not only didn't work, but it had the opposite effect? Being with me *lost* you the role?"

"In a way of speaking." Katie put her forehead in her hands. "I'm so sorry, Travis. I dragged you into this. It was all my stupid idea from the beginning. I owe you the biggest apology. I feel awful."

I was barely listening as I stared at her in amazement. I said, "This is the best news I've heard since—well, yesterday."

She lifted her head. "What do you mean? You aren't mad?"

I stared at her, feeling weight I hadn't known I was carrying lift off my shoulders. I suddenly felt light.

Katie and I didn't have to date for Edgar Pinsent anymore. We didn't have to date for Instagram or KatieWatch. We didn't have to date for her career or mine. We could date because we wanted to.

If she wanted to.

"Katie," I said, "will you be my girlfriend?"

She gaped at me. "I thought I was your girlfriend."

"You were. You are. But now you can be my real girlfriend all the time, not as a script. So I'm asking—the real me asking the real you. Will you be my girlfriend?"

I watched her expressive face move through its emotions. She frowned, her eyebrows went down, and then she sat up straighter. "We could be in a real relationship? We could just do that?"

"Yeah." I took her hand across the table and squeezed it. "Let me make my case before you decide."

"Travis—"

"Wait." I held up my hand. This was my chance, I could feel it. I could put everything on the line right now. If not now, when?

She might say no, but fuck it. I would never know if I didn't take the risk.

"I have news, too," I told her. "I have a new lawyer, and there's a bunch of complicated legal shit, but my lawsuits are going to work out in my favor in a big way. There's going to be a settlement, and I'll get a lot of money. The album is doing great, and I just opened for the Road Kings. You don't have to say yes because you feel bad for me, like I'm a stray dog. You don't need to resurrect my career anymore. You already have."

Katie was silent, staring at me in shock.

I continued, jumping all the way in. "So I was thinking that while you were in Budapest—I thought you were going to Budapest—I would buy a house. Something we both want, wherever you want. We make a home base. And when you got back from the shoot, you'd have somewhere to come home to. With me. I know that's crazy." She tried to protest, but I kept going, taking my shot. "It's impulsive, but you don't like your apartment anyway, so why don't we give it a try? We're both so busy, but we'd see each other more if we lived together. I wanted to ask you if you'd do it—for real, but it didn't seem like something to talk about over the phone from London. So I got on a flight." I shook my head. "It's a big deal, I know, and you probably want to think about it or let me down easy, but I wanted—"

"Yes," she said.

The air left my lungs. "Yes?"

"Yes," she said again, and then a third time, "Yes, Travis. Yes, I want to do that, for real. It sounds amazing." She smiled. "Except I'm not going to Budapest, so we can house hunt together."

I blinked hard. "Katie, I love you," I said. "You've just made my fucking life."

"I love you, too," she said, and when tears rolled down her cheeks, she grabbed a napkin and wiped at them. "Oh, shit. I make this look so good when I'm on set."

I stared at her, unable for a moment to believe that she was actually my girlfriend. This was happening. Even though we'd dated, even though we'd done—well, a lot. This was real in a different way. In the best way.

"What about your work?" I asked her as she put her napkin down. "Have you thought about what you're going to do? Will you go back to romcoms or do something else?"

"Oh, I've thought about it," she said, her eyes lighting with righteous anger. "I'm going to make romcoms. I already have one in mind."

"You do?"

"Yes. My own."

I sat up. "You mean *Loser Academy*?"

Katie nodded. "I'm going to finish it, and then I'm going to get it made. I'm going to produce it. I might even direct it, too. I've spent years on set with directors. If they can learn how to do it, then so can I." She gave me a wicked smile. "I've decided I don't want to work with Edgar Pinsent. I want to *be* Edgar Pinsent. But unlike him, I get to wake up with you every morning." She took my hand. "Travis, it isn't Edgar Pinsent who makes me happy, makes me giddy, makes me excited to get out of bed in the morning. It isn't him who makes me look forward to what's next. It never has been. I know that now. It's all you. Only you."

I leaned across the table and kissed her, and then I whispered in her ear.

"Crush it, Katie," I told her. "I want to watch."

THIRTY-ONE

Katie, Two Years Later

THE HOUSE WAS A MESS.

Parked cars overflowed from our driveway and lined the street. Music played on both sound systems, the one inside and the second one in the backyard. Voices and laughter rang from the kitchen. Lawn chairs and coolers littered the back yard surrounding the pool. Flip-flops, towels, and bottles of sunscreen were scattered on the pool's edge, all of it soaked with water. Someone downstairs made a loud call on a speakerphone. A baby cried.

Pure chaos.

I loved it.

I opened the bedroom door and came down the hall, twisting my hair up. It was a hot summer day, one of Portland's most beautiful days of the year, and I had changed out of my shorts and into a light sundress to keep cool. Pregnancy was sweaty.

Something dropped on the floor in the kitchen, and there was more laughter. "Oh, shit, you're in trouble," someone said. Someone else asked, "Where is she? We're ready."

As I came to the top of the stairs, Travis appeared at the bottom. My husband-to-be was as golden as ever, his tanned arms wound with ink, his burnished hair tousled. His blue eyes lit up when he looked up at me.

"There you are," he said. "Where did you go? Everyone's waiting."

"I'm coming," I said, starting down the stairs. "I just had to change."

"This is your party, babe." Travis met me halfway up the stairs, where he bent and gave my belly a brisk kiss. "Your day of glory. Come and bask."

"I'm basking, I'm basking." I tried unsuccessfully to wave him away as he took my arm. "Travis, I'm only five months along."

"You could trip," he pointed out. He steadied me, his warm hand on the small of my back. I stopped resisting. "I got you a chair. Come and put your feet up. I'll get you some lemonade. The party's in full swing."

Our house was big, and right now it was full. "She's here!" Travis shouted as we came down the hall, and applause went up. The first person to fling her arms around me in a hug was Ariana Waters, the nineteen-year-old star of *Loser Academy*.

Loser Academy, which I had written, produced, and directed. The movie that was the number one movie in the country for the third week in a row, making it a big summer hit.

I had finished the script while on the road with Travis's tour. Since I had an unexpected gap in my work schedule after telling Edgar Pinsent to shove it, I had gone house shopping with Travis in Portland, and then I had gone on tour with him instead of missing him. We had seen twenty cities in the USA and ten in Europe, having a blast. While he was in sound checks and performing, I wrote. I wrote on airplanes and buses and hotel rooms. I loved the script I wrote, and I banked everything on it. When it was finished and we were back home, I got it into production.

I got a lot of help from Travis's newly formed production company, which he'd created when his lawsuits started to settle. He put funds into getting *Loser Academy* made, though creatively he stayed away from it, saying that this was my project, not his.

Making *Loser Academy* was challenging—even hard. It made me rethink what I was capable of and what I wanted. I loved the final film, and more importantly, it was funny. At least, I thought so.

Now here we were. The movie had taken off immediately and was the hit of the summer. It was exciting and gratifying. So naturally, Travis and I threw a party.

We didn't throw parties often, but we had a beautiful house with a pool. We had lots of friends. We had something to celebrate. After finishing *Loser Academy* and the tour, Travis and I had started a new project—a baby. So far, the new project was going great.

Edgar Pinsent had made his movie, of course. It was serious and boring, and someone else played the skinny dead girl. It won Oscars. I didn't care, because I had made my own movie, and now I was throwing a party celebrating its success.

Aside from Arianna, most of the cast of *Loser Academy* was here, along with some of the production and the crew. The Road Kings had come with their wives. Finn and Juliet were here with their baby daughter. Will Hale and his wife, Luna. Andy Rockweller had come from L.A. with Elena, who he had finally married for the second time. Being Travis's go-to stylist had revived Elena's career, and she was elegantly lounging in the pool at the moment, wearing a ten thousand dollar swimsuit and looking like a queen.

As I walked to the kitchen, greeting everyone, I felt someone's arm loop through mine. From the smell of perfume, I immediately knew who it was. "We need to talk," Stella said confidentially in my ear. "The scripts are piling up. When you're done with this—" she motioned vaguely to my baby bump—"you'll be able to take your pick of projects."

"I'm not going to be done with this for a while," I said, motioning in turn to my baby bump. "And you know I'm writing another script."

"Which is wonderful, honey, just wonderful," she said soothingly. "I'm sure your next project will be a hit. But you need a backup plan, and we need to think long term. We need a strategy."

"Not today," I said with a laugh. "It's a party. Go have fun with your husband. Have a snack and a drink. Swim."

"Fun is not what we have," Stella said. She and Jonathan had gotten married in Maui three months ago, to no one's surprise. Travis and I kept getting phone calls in which they were suspiciously together and knew too much about each other. Apparently they thought they were being discreet.

"I think Jonathan is going swimming," I said to Stella. "Which means he's wearing a bathing suit."

"Fine, I'll go watch," she said, letting go and vanishing toward the backyard.

An arm slung loosely around my shoulders. It was Denver Gilchrist, the lead singer of the Road Kings.

I suppressed a happy little shiver and tried to look cool about it. I had met the Road Kings often at their studio while Travis worked on his second album. RKS was like a second home, if your second home was full of talented, unreasonably hot men. It was hard not to get giddy when Denver Gilchrist—

dark-haired, gray-eyed, gorgeous, and dreamy—slung his arm around your shoulders like an old friend.

"Great party, Katie," he said in that beautiful voice of his. "There's a seat of honor for you over here. We set it up so you don't have to do anything at this party. Just relax and soak it in." He leaned down and said in a flirty voice, "Has anyone ever told you that you look especially beautiful pregnant?"

"You do," said Axel de Vries, who was setting up a tray of snacks on the kitchen counter. He winked at me. "You really do."

I knew what this was. I *did* look beautiful pregnant—that was true. But the guys were flirting with me to piss off Travis. I turned to look at Travis and saw that it was working. He was giving us a narrow-eyed laser stare.

I elbowed Denver in the ribs. "Knock it off. Could you *not* be rivals, just for a day? You've worked together for two years now."

"It's so fun to make him mad, though." Denver sighed and dropped his arm from my shoulders. That made me sad, so I sat in the chair they had reserved for me and ate some chips. Denver handed me a glass of cold lemonade. And as instructed, I soaked it in.

It was a great party. Neal Watts's toddler son, Sam, splashed in the pool with his teenaged big sister, Amber, and the other *Loser Academy* girls. Gwen—who had agreed to work for me full time, which was a big commitment for her—sat at the edge of the pool in a vintage-style bathing suit that of course she pulled off. Stella and Jonathan talked business with the Road Kings' agent, Angie.

I watched Travis and Finn sip beers and make each other laugh at an inside joke. Those two had become like brothers over the last two years, working on each other's albums and writing songs. They not only wrote songs for their own projects, but for other artists, too. Lately they'd been on a creative streak, and apparently when they collaborated, they knew how to write hits, because bigger and bigger artists were coming to them for songwriting work.

As the party wound down, Travis stepped behind me and gently rubbed my shoulders, his talented hands working into the muscles. I groaned in pleasure.

He let go and leaned down, putting his arms around me from behind in an unapologetic hug. I soaked in the warmth of his familiar body, his scent. This man I trusted more than anything, who I had built a life with, who I was building a family with. This man who had become everything to me without even trying.

He kissed the side of my neck. "Hey," he said softly to me. "I love you."

I leaned back, soaking it in.

"I love you, too," I told him. "For real."

Printed in Great Britain
by Amazon